Bridget's Home

By Katie M. Hill

Rooks' Nest Books

Published by LuLu

The author would like to thank her friends and family for their support and encouragement during this book's writing, with a special note of gratitude to Nathaniel whose assistance in getting the manuscript print-ready finally made Bridget's story a reality.

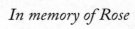

In memory of Rose

PREFACE

Long ago they were here, and their tale is a tale that was told before you and I were born, and it will be told long after you and I are returned to the earth. For they are part of the earth, and their tale is as old as the earth. It is a tale that must be told as long as the earth will last...

It was only fitting that my life's work started on the eve of the Fourth of July. I was one of a hundred people assembled on the village common, facing the graveyard. There under the stone-laden soil laid farmers and mill workers, soldiers and their families, native sons and immigrants. From behind a willow tree a mourning dove cooed as the sun set over the gravestones.

A collective gasp was heard from the audience.

I sighed with relief as the last bit of applause signaled the end of a community production of *Our Town*. As a newcomer to a small New England village, I thought the proximity of a white clapboard church, a town common (complete with a bandstand!) and an early American graveyard comprised the perfect setting for Thornton Wilder's classic play. How could such an inspiration turn into a director's nightmare? Two of the leads quit three weeks before the opening. More than one actor couldn't remember lines and/or blocking. My seven-year-old daughter became a magnet for black flies, while her pig-piling four-year-old brother broke his arm during a rehearsal. And need I mention the costume malfunctions, missed rehearsals - and, more annoying than a dropped cue - the nightly battles with mosquitoes?

An audience member congratulated me after the show.

"Marvelous job, Katie! What do you plan on doing next?"

What a question to ask! The only thing I wanted to do next was to get myself a drink and a long midsummer night's sleep. But then a picture flashed into my mind like a waking dream. It was a vision of Irish emigrants fleeing their homeland and crowding onto ships bound for America. The scene was so realistic, I could almost hear them speaking to me:

"Tell our story."

The next day, I began to read anything I could about 19th century Irish immigrants. Despite having Hibernian ancestry, the only thing I remembered about Irish immigration was a sentence or two in US History 101 about the potato famine. As I would learn, there were a lot more reasons for the Irish Diaspora than a fungus. But I will let the emigrants speak for themselves.

- K. Hill, 2011

Chapter I.

Galway

The following recollections are from the life of Moira Culligan, who emigrated from Ireland in the 1820s. They are taken from interviews conducted in 1873 by her granddaughter, Rose Haggerty:

For the centennial commemoration of the town of Cherryfield, Massachusetts, my History teacher issued an assignment to collect stories from our elderly citizens. Most of my classmates chose prominent people: clergymen, mill owners, bankers, etc. I decided to choose an ordinary person who in her life did an extraordinary thing: she left her family and friends in Ireland to begin a new life in our country.

This account is the result of numerous conversations with my maternal grandmother, Mary Culligan (whom I call "Nana") during her 73rd year. Although she is in frail health of late, she remains steadfast in her devotion to the old Irish rule of hospitality. Even when I arrive at her door unexpectedly, Nana invariably makes a strong cup of tea and offers me a currant cake still warm from the oven.

She takes pride in her housekeeping and in her appearance, displaying no evidence of stains or creases in her neatly mended flannel skirts. My grandmother smells of laundry soap and potato starch, relics of a lifetime spent bending over a washtub. Her chapped hands, weathered skin and darkly shadowed eyes betray a life of hardship. There is often a catch in her voice when she speaks of times gone by.

N.B: For purposes of clarity as well as my grandmother's fear of sounding unschooled, I have made some changes in her narrative, although I have tried to retain many of the linguistic idiosyncrasies of her conversational English.

–R.H.

All I ever wanted was a home; just a wee cottage. One with a generous hearth so the family could gather around it to share some warmth and a few heroic tales while the disappointed wind teased at our door. A simple place, sure, but a place to rest body and soul after a hard day's work. Now is that too much to ask of Life - or of God?

I hadn't set out to leave Ireland. Certainly not to come to America. True, when I had 16 summers on me I was of a mind to leave home, but not to emigrate. I just wanted to have me own household and a husband. 'Tisn't the same as here, you see. These Yankee girls marry late. Where I came from, if you didn't have a prospect by the time you were 16, well, you might as well be put up on the shelf!

And could you blame me now for wanting to leave that dark, damp, overcrowded cabin? The Sullivans lived in two rooms, all eighteen of us (for I had 15 brothers and sisters). I was the fourth child; the second daughter. Besides us there were the other creatures. We had hens sharing space with us, and in most years a pig in the lean-to. In the countryside, the pig was known as the "gentleman who paid the rent," since the whole purpose of his being there was to be fattened up and sold at market to pay the landlord when it came due.

Mind you, ours was no better nor worse than many a home on the estate. For we all lived close together near the Big House of Lord Wentworth. The old lord was not as bad as some landlords, although we had to bow to Himself and his lady whenever we met on the road. I didn't mind paying him respect, but Her Ladyship was a snob who cared only for her son, and spoiled rotten he was, too!

At two rooms, our home was the next best thing to a cottage. We had the one room with the hearth where Mam and Da slept with the latest infant in the cradle. There was always a baby in the cradle. And if anyone dare call the Irish lazy, I 'd like to show them me Mam. In me mind's eye to this day, I never see that poor woman sitting upright, for she was always bent over the cradle, or over the hearth, or over her work. In the evening, when the work was done and the neighbors would come in for *craic* (what you'd call "socializing,") Mam would be bent over from her aching back. Sure the work was hard upon us all.

In the largest room slept me brothers. Nine of them on a straw tick on the floor. 'Twas an earthen floor, though 'twas polished smooth as stone from the tramping of so many feet. Sometimes when the thatch was weak the rain could turn the floor to mud, so we were always careful to mind the roof. But with or without a leaky thatch, the house was damp from the soft rain and moist winds coming off of Galway Bay. It left a dank smell of mud mixed in with the sweat and manure and our unwashed bodies. For as much as we wanted to be clean, 'twas impossible under those conditions. We had to walk quite a ways to get to the well, and even then we'd be carrying back just enough water for cooking. The turf fire masked the odors, but not completely.

We had but one window, so what light we had came from the fire and the whitewashed walls. The kitchen was hazy from the smoke, since we had no proper chimney for it to escape. Still, our home life was centered on the hearth. We huddled about it morn and night, for it warmed our aching bones.

You can be sure that there was little in the way of furnishings. An old oaken chest, a couple of stools, rough planks that served as a table, straw ticks for beds, and the cradle. The walls were whitewashed and on them we'd hung up an old print of the Sacred Heart, a St. Brigid's cross, and creel baskets made of stiff reeds. We used those baskets to collect the turf for the fire or for gathering the dulse, the seaweed that we used on the fields for fertilizer.

Knocknadough, in the parish of Spiddal, County Galway was where we lived. Many a man there made his living from the sea, but those of us who lived inland farmed on the lands we rented from Lord Wentworth. We grew corn - by that I'm not after talking of maize like the Indians eat, but of grains such as wheat, oats, barley. All of that was shipped to England for sale in their markets. For ourselves we were given a small plot of land and the food to grow on it as well: potatoes. Sure we grew some cabbages and onions and sometimes we had a few eggs to eat, but there were always potatoes. They were cheap to raise and they did fill up our bellies so that we didn't mind not having meat except at the Christmas time, when Da would kill a hen. In some years, blight would mean small yields and scarcity, which might be why we never dared to complain about our food when we had it - leastways not out loud!

All told, we ate about ten pounds of praties a day. Sometimes I could barely stomach another boiled potato (for 'twas how they were usually cooked) but I knew that they kept us healthy and fit to work. Sure we all enjoyed good health, brothers and sisters alike, but every day you'd wake up in the morning and there was your breakfast waiting for you: potato, boiled. And when the hunger came on you in the middle of the day, there 'twas again: potato, boiled. Sure that's a bit monotonous! 'Tisn't any wonder that since coming to this country, I'm after eating Carolina rice every chance I get!

Well now, I had two older brothers, Mike and Seamus. They were working in the fields with me Da when I was still at Mam's teat. The other boys were infants when I was nearly grown, but me sisters were closer in age, so 'twas with them that I kept company when we were not helping Da in the fields or Mam with the babies.

Ah, the sisters! Six of them there were. We all slept up in the loft. There was but one older than me - Eileen. Now how can I describe such a one as herself? She was comely enough in the face with her large green catlike eyes and curling chestnut locks, but she thought she was born in the world for two purposes: the first, to tell everyone what to do. For didn't she rise before anyone else in the morning, just to give us our orders for the day?

"Finula, go help Mam with the baby!"

"Declan, get your finger out of yer nose an' go help Da in the field!"

The other thing about that Eileen was that she thought she was put on earth to tell everyone his faults. As Da would say, "Now Eileen, what man wants to hear about his faults before he's wed?" But she wouldn't listen. No man could meet her standards of perfection. One was too short, another's nose was too big, or his feet too clumsy or his eyes too crossed. They were all scared of her, the lads were. In truth, I was, too, since I often bore the brunt of her sharp tongue and hot temper.

Under the circumstances, no man in his right mind nor those in the wrong wanted anything to do with Eileen. You might wonder what this has to do with me. Plenty! In Ireland in those days, the youngest did not wed afore the eldest. 'Twasn't the custom.

Now when I was sixteen, I wanted a prospect at least, but I was beginning to fear I'd be condemned to spinsterhood, for me oldest sister already had nineteen years on her and not a bridegroom in sight.

Eileen was known around the village for going about with the air of a duchess. But since she had not the dulcet tones of a lady but the harsh voice of a crow, as well, the lads looked the other way whenever they got near her. I'd never have a chance to say a word to them, for they'd avoid me as well for fear I'd be the same. Of course, if a man were after speaking to me, I wouldn't know what to say to him, so surprised would I be that someone noticed me at all! Unlike Eileen, I was not a beauty, you see. With hair the color of a dead leaf, eyes the shade of dishwater, and a voice that never wavered above a whisper in those days, how could I ever attract notice? Besides, whenever someone did pay me heed, the clumsiness came over me. I'd trip or drop things or walk into walls. Sure the prospect of a marriage was desperate, I thought.

So 'twas on Beltane - May Day- when I had sixteen years on me, that I awakened me fifteen - year old sister, Finula, whilst the moon was still guarding the sky. "Finula," I whispers to her, "we must go outside afore the sun comes up to bathe in the morning dew!" 'Twas an old pagan custom and the priest might frown upon it, but 'twas to preserve our youthful complexions that we bothered with it, you see.

Finula had a creamy complexion but I was cursed with splotches of freckles. The day was already fair. I remember it after all these years as if 'twas yesterday. Even before the sun rose, the rich green of the grass and sunny brightness of the yellow gorse promised a brilliant start to the summer. And a dawn as pink as a maiden's blush was creeping up over the stony mountains. I'd never known a day with such beauty in it.

We were rolling downhill in the moistened grass, stark naked. I hope this doesn't shock you, but we were a lot more accustomed to such things back home than you young ones are, here in America.

All of a sudden Finula whispers, "Moira, there's a man coming up the road!" And oh, didn't we scramble behind the bushes, hurrying to put on our clothes! I did manage to steal a glance at the stranger through the branches. What a sight to behold! He was dressed in a bright blue spencer, a pink floral waistcoat and brown moleskin trousers - the clothes of an English navvy. But 'twas more than that did catch me eye. Handsome he was, with hair the color of a fox's coat, eyes green as emeralds, big broad shoulders, and hands that looked as though they were made for the work. For as I used to tell your own mother, "If a man has good strong hands upon him, he'll be a good provider an' you'll never starve."

"Who is he?" Already, I was after thinking he was far above any of the local lads in his comely appearance.

But Finula wasn't in the least bit curious. "Moira, we must get inside! The sun is after peakin' up by the hills an' the *sidhe* could steal us away, it bein' Beltane." We had the fairy faith on us still, and we regarded the first of May as the traditional start of summer, a day when the magic of the *sidhe* was particularly powerful. Who had not heard of a maiden being spirited away by the wee folk at such times?

Perhaps the stranger was one of the *sidhe* himself, I got to thinking. But didn't we learn later that day from Assumpta McQuirk - that old gossip! - that the man's name was Barnard Culligan. Sure he was her own nephew just come back from England. His family had emigrated there in '96. He was raised in London and barely remembered the country where he'd been born; 'though as he told me later, he had always wanted to come back to Ireland someday. As far back as Barnard Culligan could remember his Mam spoke of it endlessly.

Then came the day when Assumpta sent the letter to him, asking for help with the planting and the harvesting, for wasn't she was recently widowed with no man to help her save for Cousin Cornelius, and himself trampin' about the countryside playin' music.

"An' as soon as the priest finished readin' Barnard the letter, he returned to Ireland," says the Widow McQuirk to me Mam. "Sure the family went up to London when he was but a babe. They're all dead now from the cholery, God rest their souls." 'Twas a sad that they'd died, indeed, but I confess that I was impatient to hear less of old troubles and more of the man she claimed as her sister's son.

As it turned out, I didn't set eyes on Mr. Culligan again 'til Lughnasa.

St. Padraic was a wise man. True, he converted the Irish to the Christian religion, but he knew 'twas hopeless to ask them to give up the old Celtic ways, so he just re-named their feast days to make them sound holier. Beltane became May Day, the first day of Mary's month, just as the old New Year's Eve became the eve of the Feast of All Hallows (saints), or Hallowe'en. And on 1st August, when the harvest was in but before we paid the rent to the landlord, we celebrated the feast of Lughnasa, named after the old god of light, Lugh. Sure we all practiced the old pagan customs on those special days. We just went to the Mass the next day in case there was anything we'd done the night before that needed forgiveness!

On Lughnasa there were bonfires and the Crossroads Dance. 'Tis when all the unmarried ladies (the maidens) and all the unmarried gentlemen (the bachelors) gathered on the opposite sides of the crossroads, speaking amongst themselves whilst trying to steal a glance across the way at every opportunity. The music would start, and at first we'd dance with our own kind, but eventually we 'd all get in the middle of the road and pair up, so.

And that's how I finally made the acquaintance of your Granda, Mr. Barnard Michael Culligan.

He was after dancing with every lass in attendance - including Eileen. You can believe she had plenty to say about his dancing style - or lack of it.

"OUCH!! Will ye kindly take yer foot off of me toe, ye great ape!"

"Ye fool! Ye going in the wrong direction!"

"Ye would have known the step better if ye keep yer wits about ye - but maybe ye have none to begin with!"

Sure I feared that if Mr. Culligan knew that I was of the same blood as Eileen, he'd take flight before dancing with me. Maybe that was the reason he didn't ask me 'til there were no more partners available!

Unlike me older sister, not a word would come to me when I first met your Granda, but after stumbling through the dance I thought to ask him, "An' how is your aunt keepin'?"

Now Assumpta McQuirk was near sixty at that time, and for as long as I'd known her she was convinced that she was dying. After her husband died, she was sure that her own days were numbered. She had a cousin, Corny, who lived with her off and on, but he was no help at all. He preferred to wander around the countryside playing the pipes at every wake, wedding, christening, and ceilidh. We all called him "cousin," for he'd claim relation with everyone he met; 'twas a guarantee of hospitality. Well, now, with Corny out of the house for weeks at a time, the Widow decided to send for her only nephew to work her fields as well as to help carry her coffin, for she'd had no sons of her own.

And didn't the widow recover as soon as her nephew sent for the priest! Still, your Granda decided to tarry there, for he was after having a real love for the land. He would stay and work the small - holding that his family had worked for over a hundred years, 'though 'twas a poor scrap of land, what with the soil yielding up more rocks than praties.

Barnard Culligan was a queer one to fathom. At first, he couldn't tell me enough about his life in England.

"As soon's I could walk an' talk I was after workin' as a crossin' sweeper on the streets of London," says he, "clearin' the paths for the gentry to walk on. Heaven forbid that they should soil the hems of their garments with the same dirt the commoners were steppin' on!

"Then as I got older, I did anything I could put me hands to: ditch diggin', roadwork, loadin' goods onto carts an' ships... 'Tis work that puts muscle on a man but gives him no place to call his own - a travelin' about chasin' after the jobs."

I'd been trying to think of something to say after he finished talking, so finally I asks him, "Do you think you'll go back?"

I was after kicking meself as soon as I said it, for I feared he'd say "yes"!

But instead he says, quiet like, "I hope not. 'Tis a dark, dirty place: the mud's always under your feet and the dust is after chokin' your lungs. People there are livin' in the foulest slums. 'Tis no life for anyone, not when ye can live in Ireland an breathe fresh country air."

After saying all of that, he was quiet as a Yankee at an auction. When the dance was over, he tipped his cap and then disappeared with some of the other lads. No doubt to smoke his *dudeen*, I was thinking.

All the men in those days smoked their pipes whenever they had the chance. They especially craved the *dudeen* during Sunday Mass, and often stayed out smoking from the Offertory 'til Communion.

I danced with a few other lads; all of them neighbors. They offered no more *craic* than me own brothers, so the rest of the night was far short of enchantment. I wished I could be bold like some of the other colleens and engage Mr. Culligan into some more dancing or talking. I longed to tell him how I loved to watch the mist settle over the hills in the morning. I'd confess to him that I slip out to the barn of an evening when the moon's large and white as a communion wafer to catch a fairy drinking the cow's milk I'd left in a pan. I'd be after describing for him how the Connemara fields in autumn resembled brown velvet ribbons. There were so many wonderful thoughts I wanted to share with him - if only I hadn't been so timid! And now how could I explain to such a worldly man as Barnard Culligan that I was too shy to join in the dancing on feast days or the game playing at wakes? Of course I wouldn't talk to him about such things. What might he think of me if I rambled on like that?

Once when I was very young I did join in the games and merriment at a wake. Mam's cousin Una Murphy had died in 1810. 'Twas a large wake, for Una Murphy was much loved. All of the Murphys were like that. They married happily and had big families. Una must have had a hundred children at her wake, all kin. I was playing forfeits with the wee ones and laughing more than I'd ever done in all me young life when Eileen whispers to me, "'Tis makin' a fool out of yourself ye are, with yer carryin' on like that. Yer after disgracin' the family!"

After that I didn't join in the *craic*. I just stayed quiet-like, 'though you probably find that hard to believe nowadays!

Sure as rain, after the Lughnassa dance didn't Eileen start in on me?

"I saw you givin' the come-hither to Assumpta McQuirk's nephew. Just remember, he's been to London an' back, an' he's 'seen many a pretty lass. He'll be after marryin' someone with a fairer face than yours!" In truth, I didn't think I'd made his head turn once, but didn't your Granda prove Eileen wrong and come to our house the very next day wanting to speak to me Da! And didn't Da get it all wrong, too!

"I've come to ask yer permission to be walkin' out with yer lovely daughter," your Granda tells me Da.

Of course Da had to make a show of it, looking the man all over whilst I waited in the loft above, me pulse quickening with anticipation. Finally, Da made his decision.

"Permission granted! Sure Eileen will make a fine wife for ye," he says. "An' I'll give ye a hen besides!"

I nearly fainted right then and there! Eileen betrothed to Mr. Culligan? Eileen! She of the great gob?!

So Granda straightened him out quicker than a lightening flash!

"'Tisn't Eileen I'm after askin' for! 'Tis Moira; 'tis Moira that's won me heart."

But just as I feared, me Da shook his head.

"Out of the question! 'Tisn't right for the younger to wed before the elder! Ye must wait 'til we find a match for Eileen!"

Wait! Impossible! For more years than I care to recount we waited, and all the while me youth fading along with me hopes! But after many love charms and hundreds of prayers to St. Jude, didn't our luck change! One day I was on the beach collecting dulse - what you're after calling seaweed. We spread it on the fields for fertilizer, you see. I was just about done for the day when I noticed something floating on the water. 'Twas a man, washed up ashore! At first I thought he was drowned, so I ran over to the field and fetched me brother Seamus. But

Seamus examined the man and says to me, "Not drowned! He's only hurt, Moira. Sure we should take him home."

So we carried the man between us all the way home. He was light but tall, so 'twas tiring be taking him over a mile underfoot. And when we finally got there, who's standing there at the doorway? Herself, Eileen!

"'Tis about time you got back, Moira Sullivan!" she says, "Do ye have the dulse for me?"

I didn't want to be burdened with the man another minute; I was that weary.

"I've no dulse for ye today, Eileen," says I, "but I've somethin' else instead: Here; 'tis a drowned man. You look after him; I've enough work to be doin'."

Eileen took over his care, for once not passing the job on to one of us. Sure she looked after him, she did! When the poor man came to, didn't he think Eileen was an angel, come down from Heaven to rescue him from the jaws of Death! Surely the salt water must have addled his brain!

As it turned out, Padraic Nee - the drowned man - lived but a mile or two from Spiddal, on the other side of Knocknadough. His family had been farming their land longer than the English had been in Ireland, but he got it into his head to try his hand at fishing, with disastrous results!

Well, soon as the patient was able, Da sent for the priest, and so Mr. Nee and Eileen were wed. They settled on his family farm and in short order they made me Mam and Da grandparents.

So at last I could be wed to Barnard Culligan. By then, I had so many years on me I really should have been put up on the shelf! And you can be sure that after waiting so long, all our neighbors and relations turned out for the nuptials.

We were wed on a cold, mizzly February day. I wore a new red petticoat, and Eileen (who'd become more soft-hearted in her married state) wove me a shawl of thick black wool. She and the rest of the family accompanied me in the bridal procession to me new home.

When we arrived the *craic* had already started. Padraic Nee brought poteen, Assumpta McQuirk had tobaccy and Cousin Corny played his pipes. Other neighbors gave us butter and cheese, bacon and bedding, and Lord Wentworth himself sent down ham and cakes and wine. Many a toast was made in our honor long before Fr. Coyne arrived to join us together. And weren't there hundreds of tears shed so in happiness - me own included!

Afterwards, there was dancing and more toasting. Yet no one there was disgraced from the drink, although your Granda had high spirits, indeed! He asked all of the ladies to kiss him for luck. I wasn't used to his ways, so and the green came over me, but not for long. I was enjoying the day and was flushed from the wine meself.

'Twasn't afore the frosty moon appeared in the sky that the wedding guests finally left us alone. Now all during our walking out we attended wakes where we'd play kissing games, and we stole away many a time from a party to a field or a barn, but on that night the bashfulness came over me. I sat in silence while Granda smoked his pipe. After a while he pulled me towards him and I rested me head on his big broad shoulder whilst he stroked me hair.

"Will ye always be so quiet, mavourneen?" he asks me. "Sure I don't have the talk in it for the both of us!"

Indeed, I was quiet that night, but over the years that's changed, and rare's the time now that I've been at a loss for words!

When we married we moved into a smaller cottage on the estate, near Assumpta McQuirk and Cousin Corny. The house had one very large room, a loft, and a good thatched roof that kept us warm and dry that first winter. For furnishings we had two stools, a creel, a small trunk, and a straw tick for our bed. We felt blessed indeed. All went well that first year, and I was after hoping we would be needing a cradle before the end of the second.

But 'twasn't such a grand year for the landlord, as it turned out. The prices for corn were dropping fast, and since we grew it for Lord Wentworth s own profit, 'twas decided at the Big House that our farming efforts were not "productive" enough. Things had changed at the Wentworth Estate, you see. Old Lord Wentworth, who'd always acted kindly to his tenants, had died in the early spring. His son George was after seeing to things now. Though only one and twenty, his heart was already hard as stone. His was the world of numbers and balance sheets, and people only mattered to him if they could prove their usefulness in his quest for profit. And sure we couldn't do that for him. So one day in September before the rent was due we were visited by the sheriff, who handed us the order for evictment.

Of course we couldn't read the notice, not having much in the way of book learning, so the sheriff read it to us and asked if there were any questions.

"How much time, sir?" Granda asks.

We had to be out in ten days' time, according to the notice, and if we failed to do so, our belongings would be removed and carted away.

After the sheriff left I sat in the doorway and wept; not just for meself and your Granda but also for the babe I was carrying.

"A fine world for a child to be born into, with no place to be calling its home! What will we do?"

But Granda stayed calm.

"Don't ye worry none, mavourneen. We'll walk to Galway Town."

Well word of an eviction travels fast, and within minutes after the sheriff had gone Assumpta McQuirk was at our door. She wanted us to stay with her. "What with the child comin', Moira will be needin' her kin'" she says.

Granda wouldn't hear of it! "We're leavin'. I can look after her fine by meself!"

And that ended it.

Chapter II.
The Erie

Come the day of our evictment, I took the last bit of turf from the hearth and the St. Brigid's cross off the wall, where it hung above the door for luck. I packed them carefully in a creel while Granda carried a sack in which we'd placed our pots and pans and clothes. Then I sprinkled holy water on ourselves and our belongings. I'd always kept a jar of it by the hearth, just in case. Sure if ever we needed divine protection 'twas on that day, I was thinking! And so we left our home for good or worse.

Some 15 miles fell under our feet by the time we got to Galway Town. 'Tis a large market town, and we were after hoping there might be a farmer still looking for hires. There wasn't much work to be had, though, for 'twas the autumn of the year and the harvest was in. But we spotted a man sitting behind a table, wearing a tall beaver hat and a black silken waistcoat. Sure I'll never forget the sight of that man - the girth on him! His stomach stuck out in front of him like a drum and his large head was as round as a wheel of green cheese. He had a stack of papers, a quill, and an inkwell setting on the table and there was a line of men standing in front of it. So Granda joined the line.

The man took a black segar out of his mouth and looked up and down at Granda as if he was a horse he was after buying at the fair. Sure I thought he'd ask him to open his mouth so that his teeth could be counted!

"Say!" the man shouts. His voice was louder than a cannon shot. "You look like a fine, healthy lad. Ever do any canal work - hauling, hewing, carrying?"

And Granda says, "I have, indeed. All o' that and more besides. Sure I was doin' canal work in England from the time I was a lad."

I tell you, I expected lightening to strike him dead on the spot! Granda had done many a dirty job when he lived in London, but canal work wasn't one of them. And there he was lying bald-faced to the man!

But the man didn't see through Barney's blarney! Instead he asks him, "How'd you like to come to America and build a big canal? "

So Granda asks, "Will ye pay me?"

Well the man laughed from the depths of his bulging belly! "Sure I'll pay you. I'll pay you cash wages. I'll even pay for your passage."

He noticed me standing in back of Granda and smiled. "That bonnie little lass there - she's your wife?"

"*Sea* - yes, she is," says Granda.

"She got kin to stay with here?" the man asks him.

"Yes," says Granda. "But she's comin' with me. If she can't get passage to go with me, Sir, so I won't be goin' to Americay. We won't be parted."

"Well then, if you feel that way about it, I will pay for her passage, too. You have my word."

The man leaned across the table and handed Granda a piece of paper and a quill. "Well, whaddya say, Paddy? Just sign right here."

Granda glanced at the paper for a moment, then at me. But I didn't know what to be telling him! I knew no more about America than I did about the moon! But after a bit of thinking about it he took the quill and made his mark on the paper.

The man said to meet him there the next day and all would be arranged.

"But how do we know we can trust this man?" I says to Granda.

"An' why shouldn't we?" he says. "Amn't I desperate to find work? We'll go, mavourneen - an' I want no arguments!"

In truth, I was half hoping the man wouldn't buy me passage ticket. I loved Galway - not the big town but the countryside where I'd lived all me life. Even though our house was no longer there, our people remained. Finula had just become betrothed to a neighbor boy, and Eileen just given birth to her second son. Me brothers Declan and Mike were coming home soon from working in England, and I wanted to watch all the others grow up. I also wanted our baby to have grandparents nearby. There were so many reasons why me heart was tied to home.

We stayed at a cheap lodging that night, and I stayed awake as the hours passed, wondering if this was the right thing for us to be doing. For how could we be leaving our friends, and our family and our country, knowing we'd never return?

But we were desperate, we were, and we went to the port at dawn. The man was waiting there, just as he'd promised, but didn't he still try to talk Granda out of taking me with him!

"The Erie is no place for a woman," the man says to Granda.

"But I told you yesterday that I won't go without her!"

The man could see that Barnard Culligan was not one to be crossed, so he paid for me ticket and then escorted us to the ship.

"Good luck to you, Mrs. Culligan," he says, "you will need it." Oh, if only we realized the truth in that!

We sailed from Galway to Liverpool in England, and from there we had to wait a few days for our ship. I tell you now, I wouldn't wish that trip on me worst enemy! Those were the days before steam, when a ship was swift if it took less than eight weeks to reach America. For us it was near seven down there in the belly of the ship - the steerage - with hardly a foot of space above our heads. The whole time there was many a storm at sea, it being the autumn of the year. The ship was after tossing and turning on the waves and - oh! - wasn't me stomach tossing and turning along with it! Was I ever sick! I had the puke bucket beside me the whole time, even when we sat down at the long table to eat the stirabout that they gave us for our meals. As the ship listed from side to side, the bowls of porridge would slide across the table. There was many a passenger like me, though, who'd just as soon it landed on the other side!

Well now, the less said of that voyage the better. What helped me to get through it, besides prayers, was the thought of breathing fresh air again.

We landed in the city of New York.

Fresh air?! The smoke was as thick as wool and the air was dense with the talking of so many people. Indeed, they talked very fast!

"What tongue is it they 're after speakin'?" I asks Granda.

"Why, 'tis English," he tells me.

I tell you, 'twas like no English I'd ever heard, the way they were after speaking it in New York!

There were more people walking about in New York City than I ever imagined there could be on this earth, and there were almost as many horses, pulling carts and carriages, as there were people. Those horses were galloping so fast you had to be quick in order to avoid getting run over by the beasts.

And what a noisy place, 'twas that city! There were bells ringing, children crying, dogs barking - and street hawkers singing of their wares. Sure everyone in New York has to be selling you something! One man held a string of fish in me face, soon's I stepped off the ship.

"Fresh fish today! Want to buy some fish?" Fresh, he called it - and by the stink of it you'd think 'twas old as Methuselah!

That was it for me. "I don't like it here," I says to Granda. "It's too fast, too loud, too dirty - an' it reeks! Sure the ship's still there in the harbor. Let's go back to home."

But your Granda just shook his head.

"Home? What home, Moira? From now on, this is our home, an' we must make the most of it!" Sure, he was enjoying all the sights and sounds of the big city.

"Over there, mavourneen! They're sellin' apples. An' will ye look at the poltroon there, smokin' his pipe! An' aren't there some lovely ladies in this city- much prettier than the English ladies." Granda was always one to notice a beautiful woman. He was after tipping his dirt-dusted hat to every one of them.

Lucky for us we didn't have to stay in New York City for long. An agent came to fetch us and take us up north. But before leaving the city we were treated to a meal at an inn at the canal company's expense. What a feast! There was roast mutton, apple pie, turnips and potatoes and warm white flour bread soaked with butter. I had never seen so much food on a table in me whole life. I didn't think I 'd have to eat again for a month, at least!

The agent brought us by coach to the Erie Canal, which your Granda would help to build. 'Twas quite an undertaking, digging that canal. Dangerous, hard work. Many a good man died in the attempt. But Granda had fear of neither dirt nor death.

Most of the workers lived along the Erie in boarding houses or company cabins. They were a mixed lot. Some were from Ireland, some from England, Germany, Scotland, and, of course, America. I'd not be telling the truth if I said they got along all the time. There was a lot of hard drinking in the off times and because of it there was a lot of hard fighting, too. I will say, though, that when there were jobs to be done, they all worked like well-matched teams of oxen.

The days passed quickly enough. Granda was hauling stones for one of the hardest jobs in the canal: blasting through the great rocks at Lockport. We were lucky, sure, because 'twas such a big undertaking that he had work in the winter as well. All year 'round he was after taking away the debris out of huge craters that were formed from the blasting. Sure the noise from all the explosions was beyond deafening! Plates would fall off the shelves and no matter how much I expected it I was taken by surprise every time.

While the canal work was going on we boarded with a German family; the Muellers. Mr. Mueller and his grown son were skilled masons who came over to do the stonework.

His wife was a gentle, quiet, and kindly woman. She was me midwife when the time came. I was frightened, I was, but Mrs. Mueller stayed calm - until she found out there were twins.

"Mien Gott!" she cries, "Two of them, both girls - and both very pretty, like their mutter".

That's why your Mam is named Kathleen. I was after calling her that because Mrs. Mueller's name was Katrina, and it means the same thing in German as the Irish Caitlin-Kathleen. Of course Granda thought both the girls should have American names, and he hated it when I named your aunt Siobhan. "We live in America, an' she'll have an American name - Jane! An' I want no arguments!" I was still after calling her Siobhan. She's never complained about it, though she calls herself Jane.

Mrs. Mueller only spoke a little English, and 'twas in fear of being misunderstood that she was not talkative. Sure I sometimes think it made her seem diffident. Of course your Granda took that silence as a challenge. She was plain, grey - haired and plump as a pigeon, but whenever he saw her, he'd make a fuss, bowing down to kiss her hand just like a Frenchman.

"Sure the sun in the sky 'tisn't half as radiant as your very youthful countenance, Frau Mueller," he'd tell her, and the old woman would blush like a schoolgirl.

"Ach, Mr. Culligan, you iss so very charming, but a bit ofa rascal, I sink!"

Even when the canal was finished the noise continued, because there were celebrations from Rochester to New York City, and Lockport was no exception. I recall that crisp October morning back in '25 when Granda awakened me in a great state of excitement.

"Get the babies and yerself ready, Moira. Forget about the washin' up for once! Sure the parade will be startin' an' I want to be right out in front!"

Oh what a grand day that was altogether! There were gun salutes and a parade and fireworks - the first I'd ever seen. Sure I thought there was nothing else in the world even half as lovely! And of course there were a lot of fancy-sounding speeches. What a great thing 'twas for Granda to be one of the workers that the politicians were after praising for their part in the project! "Hewers of stone and haulers of water," someone called them. That made Granda especially happy. In truth, I believe he felt the *craic* was just for himself, he was that proud of his role in building the Erie.

The day after the big event Mrs. Mueller held a little celebration at the boarding house. She'd roasted a goose and Mr. Mueller served their best home-brewed beer. He offered up a toast.

"To Herr and Frau Culligan: May you be not only doubly blessed but triply blessed with kinder!"

The Muellers were good to us. Like a Mam and Da they were. Themselves being Catholics, they served as godparents to the girls. I tell you, they loved those babies as if they were their own grandchildren. Sure they'd have spoilt them if your Granda allowed it! I miss them to this day. But the work on the Erie was coming to an end, and so was our life in New York.

Thus ended the first interview with my grandmother. She said she couldn't remember much more about those early days on the Erie: "'Tis too long ago for an old woman to recollect," she laughed. I could see that she was fatigued, so I took my leave. I promised to come again soon, and she smiled. "Better sooner than later," she said.

Chapter III.
Worcester

When I visited my grandmother a week later, we picked up the narrative where we had left off, as if I had only been gone out of the room for a few minutes instead of seven days. She poured tea and commenced by telling me of her early days in Worcester.

How did we come to Massachusetts, you ask? 'Twas like this: When the job on the Erie Canal was done, Granda was one of the workers who was asked to come down here to help dig the Blackstone Canal. 'Twas Toby Boland who told him to come with him to Massachusetts.

"They are needing some good hard workers to dig a canal from Worcester to Providence," he tells Granda. "The wages are $9 a month and a pint of rum a day - the Yankees are used to having the rum while they work."

Mr. Boland himself had worked on the Erie, but he was now helping the Yankee bosses in recruiting workers for the Blackstone. There were 30 men who followed Toby Boland down to Worcester.

Once we arrived, Mr. Boland found us lodging in a room above O'Toole's Dry Goods Store on Tatnuck Street. You'd hardly believe Quentin O'Toole was one of us by the looks of him. His waistcoat was of the softest green wool, and a stock starched stiff as a day-old corpse corralled his neck.

Sure his blood-red cravat was but a mirror for his florid complexion. And a well-fed man he was, too, judging from the size of his jowls!

In his white-gloved hands Quentin O'Toole carried a walking stick that was made from an old oak branch, the top of which forked in a fashion that gave it the appearance of the devil's own pitchfork. But from where we stood, he was no fiend from hell but a kindly shopkeeper with a place for us to rest our weary heads. And when he spoke, the green fields of Tipperary rolled over his tongue.

"I started here sixteen years ago with nary a penny in me pocket and now I own a dry goods store, several properties, and some shares in the canal!" So he told us. 'Twas but a few months later that we'd hear from one of his tenants that Mr. O'Toole came to this country with more than a few pennies in his pocket, since he was after being the son of a merchant. But as he'd probably make of it, a tale of rising up from humble beginnings was what our people needed to hear -especially if they were to become his future customers.

"Well now, Mr. Culligan," he says to Granda," I'll let you a room at a very reduced rate. You don't have to be thanking me, now. 'Tis good for business after all."

Those were fine days when Granda was working the Blackstone. Worcester was a growing town in the middle of Massachusetts, and a lot of its growth seemed to be coming from our own countrymen. They came to dig the canal and stayed on to work on the railroad. There was a bustling town center, and around that snaked the railway tracks with rows of shacks surrounding them. (Amongst the Yankees, the shacks were called "paddy camps" since 'twas our own people, the "paddies," living in them). On Worcester's shadier streets the rich lived in two-story mansions, and in the outskirts was farmland with rich soil - for New England. For as you know, in most places around here the rocks stick out of the thin soil like weeds. It always puts me in mind of Connemara.

We were soon settled into a small room. Quentin O'Toole was involved in plenty of construction projects and owned several properties in Worcester, including four apartment buildings, two saloons - and any other building he could get his hands on, either for fixing up or tearing down. From the buildings that were torn down he got the furnishings for his boarders' rooms, including our own. Just a few pieces of furniture, mind you: a bed, a small cot for the babies, a chest, three chairs with a matching table, and a redware washbasin. Perhaps you'd think our room was stark, considering all of the draperies and looking glasses and horsehair sofas that Americans are so fond of these days, but 'twas more than we had back in Galway, for sure.

O'Toole was always pleasant to us, he was, and he had a generous hand for newcomers, 'though it could be said that he drove as hard a bargain as any man, Irish or American. He and his wife had come over years earlier and set up a shop that rivaled any in Worcester for its large stock and great number of satisfied customers. Indeed, many a Yankee patronized his store; 'twas that good. Quentin O'Toole was well-respected amongst the native sons. Sure those Yankees admired anyone who could make a dollar. And didn't our own people adore him as well! We all knew we could rely on his help in finding a room, a meal, and perhaps a lead on a job. He was more than willing to help his countrymen, for as he would say, "'Tis good for business, after all."

But for the life of me, I could never figure out how Quentin and Teresa O'Toole ever got it into their heads to marry each other. Not that they were quarrelsome; but they were as unlike each other as salt is to sugar. He was always after looking the bon ton gentleman, while Mrs. O'Toole was the one to be starched-capped and dressed prim as a nun. 'Twas a wonder she could be so tidy, since it seemed as if every time you turned around she had another baby in her arms! She was extremely devout and was never caught without a rosary in her hand and was after caring for any sick or starving soul that came to her door. Mrs. O'Toole taught catechism to Worcester's Catholic youngsters and attended daily Mass as well as the Friday Stations of the Cross and the Wednesday night Novena. Quentin attended Mass regularly, but from the way he was after glad-handing the parishioners I was after thinking that for him, 'twas just "good for business" after all!

We lived in Worcester for two years while the Blackstone was getting dug. When the first boat, the Lady Carrington, arrived in Worcester in '28, there were cannon firings heard all over the town, and like they did with the Erie, the politicians made much of the canal workers.

Then came the next day when Granda went to work and was told by the boss:

"Canal's all done. You can go on home, Paddy."

But how were we to be getting home? Even if we wanted to, we hadn't the means to do so. We didn't have a penny to spare, truth be told. Hard times, they were. For over a year we hardly knew where the next meal would be coming from. If 'twere not for Mrs. O'Toole's daily bowls of sulphurous cabbage soup, sure we'd have starved.

'Twas in those dark days we found out the hard truth about America: there is plenty of work to be had so long as you're a native Yankee and a Protestant. Many's the time Granda went for a job, but be it brick-laying, ditch-digging - street-sweeping, even - no matter the work, he was always asked the same two questions:

First: "Where do you come from?" He'd tell them that he came from Ireland.

Next: "Does that mean that you are Catholic?" And he'd tell them he was.

Then 'twas always: "Well we don't hire Papists!"

They were hard times indeed. All we could do was pray and hope. I took care of the prayers and your Granda took care of the hope. Whenever things got too unbearable, he would take me into his arms, put me head on his shoulder, and he'd say, "Don't worry, mavourneen. 'Twill get better by and by. Someday we'll have plenty to eat, and the food will be grown by ourselves, too."

"An' how do you suppose that will happen, Barnard Culligan?" I always said that to him in a teasing way. Sure I wasn't as rosy-minded as Granda, but just hearing his dreams made me feel better, and 'twas a lot of dreaming he did in those days.

"We'll have a farm, so," he'd say. "We'll have fruit trees an' gardens an' chickens an' pigs, an' I swear upon the head of St. John the Baptist that we'll be livin' fat off the land, we will! Just be patient."

Then one day Mr. O'Toole called us down into his shop. There were only two other people in there; a man and a woman. The man was of short stature and what you might be calling portly. He wore a black waistcoat and a silken cravat and looked altogether a gentleman. The lady was wearing a grey silk bonnet with three black plumes on it and a plum-colored woolen gown. They had at least sixty years apiece on them.

"Mr. Culligan, Mr. Brewster here is looking for someone to work on his farm. I thought as how you might be interested," Mr. O'Toole says to Granda.

Interested! Interested in feeding our children? Interested in having work for our hands?

"*Sea* - em, yes, sir, we'd be very interested, thank ye," Granda answers.

So Mr. Brewster smiled - 'twasn't at all like the thin-lipped half-smiles of the Yankee patrons who came into the dry goods store, but a warm smile that caused his cheek to dimple. He had eyes as brown as butternuts and his face was tan, telling me that here was no gentleman farmer like the landlords back home but a true man of the soil. He shook Granda's hand with the grip of a man who knew his way around the plough as well as the market.

"Good to meet you, Culligan," he says. "You are not afraid of hard work, are you?"

"No, sir," says Granda. "I've always had the hard work upon me, wherever I hang me hat."

"Well, I have over two hundred acres, but you will not be working alone. There is my son and a couple of hired hands to help, and I like to work my own land when I am able."

While Granda and Mr. Brewster talked, Mrs. Brewster looked at me over her spectacles. Her eyes were blue as a calming sky, but her carriage was far from relaxed. In truth, she put me in mind of one of the stiff horsehair chairs in a priest's parlor.

"And you, Bridget...?"

"Moira, Ma 'am," I says - in a polite way, of course.

"I beg your pardon?" she asks me. I noticed she was after cupping her hand over her ear, so I nearly shouted - which I suppose doesn't sound very genteel:

"MOIRA! ME NAME'S MOIRA, AFTER THE BLESSED MOTHER!"

"Oh, I see," she says, "May I just call you Bridget? It will be so much easier to remember. "

I decided 'twould be of no advantage to disagree with her just then, what with us needing the work and all. I could always correct her later when we were safely employed, I was thinking.

"As I was about to inquire of you, Bridget: have you any experience in dairying?"

"Sure I have, ma'am," I says. "Why, wasn't milkin' the landlord's cow me own job as a child!"

"Excellent!" she says, and you 'd think I told her I had invented a mechanical cow, she seemed that impressed!

So she tells me, "We have fifty cows and we keep them in milk all year. Our cheese and butter is in demand in Boston. Of course, my daughter-in-law and her two girls run the dairy now, but I still keep my hand in it."

She smiled at me, and didn't I see some warmth in it? She assured me that she and Mr. Brewster would not treat us as servants but as "hired help" - part of the family. We were to eat together as well as work together - and we would live in the rooms above the barn. That sounded like servants' quarters to me, but I held me tongue.

"It will be just the right size for the two of you," she tells me.

That's it, I was thinking. Will she still give us a place when she finds out there are almost five of us?

But then Mr. Brewster says, "So Mrs. Culligan, your husband agrees to my offer of employment and lodging for your family. Why not gather your children while he fetches your trunks? No use idling away our time when I can put him to work!"

Mrs. Brewster stepped back from me when she heard the word "children," but she showed no sign of disapproval, and indeed, she produced a ginger drop for both of the girls when

I brought them downstairs. "Why they are so adorable, Bridget!" she says, and she seemed to mean it.

I could see there was no getting around it with me name, so "Bridget" I became from that day on, just as your Granda would have to answer to "Paddy."

The Brewsters lived in a twelve-room, two-storied home they called a "mansion house," though 'twas nowhere near as large and grand as the Big Houses of Ireland. But I wouldn't tell them that. House proud they were! Mr. Brewster had been a poor farm boy who had the good fortune to love and marry Mrs. Brewster when she was a well-to-do young widow. With her money they built his dream house. It had doors on all four sides, a sweeping staircase that split the house in two, plenty of windows, a spring-cooled dairy in the basement, and a sturdy English-style barn that housed their Merino sheep and Devon cattle. The rooms above it would be our home.

Mr. Brewster was Lord of the Acres, but 'twas Mrs. Brewster who reigned over the house, 'though her daughter-in-law, Matilda, seemed eager to nudge the old woman off the throne. Matilda was always appealing to Mrs. Brewster's vanity, convincing her that it was the fashion in Boston to have Venetian-striped carpeting, silk upholstered furniture, and fancy French wallpaper (but only in the best parlor and the dining room. Plain American was good enough for the rest of the house). The old woman didn't care for all the latest domestic inventions, though. Shortly after we came to work there, a cook stove was delivered one day, but Mrs. Brewster never did take to it. She was after burning every dinner, and one day she threatened to have Granda chop it into bits! For as long as she lived, Mrs. Brewster continued to cook over the hearth.

I got along well enough with the elder Mrs. Brewster. Sure, she was strict. At first she was always hovering about, making sure that the butter was salted enough or that I scalded the milk properly. It got on me nerves, and sometimes I had to fight back the tears. I couldn't get out of me own way for the awkwardness I was feeling, so. I'd break more dishes and spill more cream than ever; all because I was fearful that I should displease her and lose me job. She must have noticed, because one day after I had cleaned up from the cheese-making old Mrs. Brewster called me into the kitchen.

"Bridget," she says," I do not want you to feel ill at ease here. When I try to correct you about your work, it is only for your own good. You do want to learn to do things our way, I trust?"

"*Sea* - yes ma'am," I tells her.

"Well," she says, "I just wanted you to know that I think you are doing good work and that you no longer need my supervision."

"Thank you, Mrs. Brewster," I says. What a relief! Here I was thinking that she was after firing me!

But then she says to me, "Of course, my daughter-in-law will continue to guide you in the dairying."

Believe me, that news gave me no joy! Matilda Brewster watched me every minute; more than her mother-in-law ever did, the she-devil! Not a civil word passed from her tongue to me ear:

"You call this pan clean? Do it again, you lazy slut!"

"WHAT? You want to take the morning off to go to tell your sins to a Papist priest? That is of no use, Bridget. Do you not know that all Catholics are bound for hell?"

I tell you, sometimes I felt like I was in hell, for all the work that I had to do and all of the scolding I would get for not doing it up to Matilda's standards. Of course your Granda would try to soothe me by talking about that grand farm we'd be having someday. "Sure 'tis only for a short while until we get our own land. Be patient," he would tell me. But 'twas hard to imagine ever getting away from there.

In those early years, 'twas Granda who would be looking at the bright side of the penny. He loved working in the fields and the fresh air was a tonic to him, so no matter how back-breaking the work, he was happy to do it. Both of the Brewster men, father and son, respected him, and all the Brewster women loved him. He could even bring a smile to the stony face of Matilda Brewster; especially since he would pay her compliments whenever he passed her.

"Surely the loveliest rose in your garden pales beside your own beauty, Ma'am!" That was one of his favorites! He would try to look sincere, but there was always a twinkle in his eyes.

Of course Matilda would pretend not to like the flattery. "Really, Paddy, enough with your blarney!" But you could tell she loved it. And the old Mrs. Brewster blushed like a giddy young girl whenever Granda would kneel down and kiss her hand! To this day, I can scarcely believe he got away with such boldness!

But whilst Granda could charm his way around Matilda, all I was after getting from her lips was orders to work, work, work and work harder all the time, at that. 'Twas endless! Sure the worst was our first Christmas in that house, when instead of going to Mass, Matilda told me I had to dip one hundred candles because the old Mrs. Brewster was too sick with a cold to help her. I was after thinking that she was just determined that I wouldn't celebrate the "heathen" holiday, as she called it.

That Christmas Eve, Granda wanted to put a candle in the window to guide the Christ Child, as we did in Ireland.

"Do as you like," I says, "but why would He want to go to a place where people refuse to celebrate His birth?"

Well now, I was after going to bed as early as the children that night; I was that downhearted, when I heard footsteps coming up the stairs.

"Probably she's after bringin' me her dirty laundry to do as well," I says to your Granda. I didn't say it in jest, believe me.

But instead of the beak-nosed Matilda, who comes into the room but the old man, carrying a bundle not of dirty clothes, but of a turkey and the trimmins!

"Merry Christmas!" he says. "I know how important a day it is to you people. Please accept our compliments for the season. Oh, and you may both take a half day tomorrow."

Sure your Granda was beside himself with glee! "Imagine that," he says. "Our first Christmas gift in Americay, an' from a Yankee at that!"

Two months after Christmas we had another gift. Our first boy (your Uncle Pat) was born on St Bridget's Day, the first of February. I was hoping to have a midwife or even one of the Brewster women to help, but instead, Mr. Brewster paid his own physician, Dr. Brigham, to do the delivery. Like the turkey at Christmas, the old man told us that the doctor's services "were not to be deducted from your wages."

Now whenever Matilda Brewster was not at home, I worked alongside her two daughters, Hannah and Tirza. Tirza was pretty and charming, but she knew it! She had a merry laugh and golden locks, which she dressed up with ribbons. Sure the poor girl was without the sense of a flea. She was forever losing things and asking me to help her find them "before Mother finds out." At least once a day during me first year at the Brewsters' I had to search for hair combs, ribbons, lockets, shoes, and once even a petticoat, which had fallen off her fashionably small waist right onto the road!

Despite her lack of common sense, Tirza was not at a loss for beaux. That was what she called all the moony-faced young men who wrote her love letters and took her for sleigh rides. If she were a flower, sure she would have been a catchfly, like the ones in the Brewsters' pleasure garden that lured flies into its lovely scented trap. Many was the night I was awakened from me sleep by a knock at our door. Tirza would come in very late after a ball or a sleigh ride or whatever else she did in terms of courting, but she feared her father's wrath.

"Bridget, could you let me in? I will just die if Father sees me coming home at this hour!" From our rooms above the barn the girl could cross over to the second floor landing and creep into the chamber she shared with Hannah.

Sure I would try to scold her. "Tirza, 'tis the last time I let you in. A disgrace, you are, stayin' out so late!"

But she would look up at me round-eyed, with a smile that kept company with the dimple on her chin. "Oh please, Bridget, I promise you this is the last time!" And so I would give in, even though she would be begging me to let her in for the "last time" the very next night.

Now Tirza had eyes for no one in particular until she met Joshua Spencer of Atlanta, Georgia. During our second winter with the Brewsters they decided to host a George Washington's Birth Night Ball. Winter was a time when many a country family entertained, what with the harvest and butchering being finished. The doings were to take place up in the old ballroom, which had been serving as bedchambers for the Brewsters' children. When the older Brewster boys, Jed and Abijah, were home from college they slept with their younger brothers, Jacob and Zeke, on one side of the room, and on the other side, divided by a partition, there was a bed for Tirza and Hannah. The room was so large that Matilda Brewster kept her quilt frame set up in it, 'though she was rarely after hosting a quilting frolic. Too afraid the other ladies might gossip about her afterwards, no doubt!

The preparations for the ball got underway right after the New Year. Indeed, Tirza fussed over the invitations. She had a lovely hand and was given the task of writing them up. It was deciding on the guests that caused her fair head to spin. Each day the list grew longer and longer until Mr. Brewster was afraid he would have to put some of the guests in the root cellar!

Hannah was after slaving over the new frock she was making for the fete. I had never seen the poor girl so distraught. At least once a day she would ask me for advice on a sleeve or a furbelow. Thanks be to St. Patrick that she never asked me opinion of the color, for 'twas a mustard yellow that made her look bilious. Musha, the poor girl was plain enough without wearing something that would make her look even homelier! But to Hannah, the color was like cloth of gold because it came from Boston. Eliphet Brewster was after buying it for Matilda, but she said it put her in mind of a crooked necked squash! Truth be told, though, Hannah did make the gown look smart. She was skilled with the needle indeed. And didn't I know she wanted to show off her dressmaking talents for a certain Dr. Turner, for though she'd fancied the man for two years he had never given her the time of day.

Matilda Brewster made Tirza's gown. Or I should say gowns? Sure the girl had three silken dresses for her choosing, and still she was far from satisfied. "After all, I must be *la plus belle femme dans la chambre* that night," she says to me one day.

She was always after spouting French words in order to let everyone know that she'd attended Academy.

I thought my job was over for the day after I finished setting up the ballroom. With Granda's help I dismantled the beds and quilt frame, dusted the room, and set up the chairs and tables for the ball. We planned to spend the night in our rooms but later that afternoon old Mr. Brewster himself knocked on our door.

He was leaning on his cane. He had the gout, you see. The man lived high off the hog, eating his share of cakes and cream and drinking a lot of flip. No temperance man was old Mr. Brewster!

"Are you not coming to the ball?" he asks.

"Are we invited?" asks your Granda.

Mr. Brewster laughed, so, and told us that of course we must come. "And bring the children, too." He had a soft spot for the wee ones; always giving them sweets and letting them jump in the haystacks. A kindly man was old Mr. Brewster.

So I put on me best frock- the only one that had not been mended within a stitch of its life - and Granda changed into his other pair of trousers. We brought the twins and little Pat with us into the ballroom, though they soon tired and needed to be put to bed.

In those times, before that prig of a queen in England made frivolity the eighth deadly sin on both sides of the water, the old ones knew how to throw a hooley! The sounds of the fiddle took me right back to Connemara, and the young ones stepped lively to the music. Mr. Brewster Sr. cut quite a figure when he danced with his wife and all the other ladies - especially the young, pretty ones. Even Matilda took in a dance with her husband and seemed to enjoy it!

Granda and I sat behind the punch bowl, tapping our feet to the music. We were after thinking of dancing ourselves when who comes up to me but the old man, bowing to me and asking, "Mrs. Culligan, may I have the honor?"

Well now me face must have been as red as a beet! Mr. Brewster led me over to the dance floor and guided me through "Money in Both Pockets." His brow was drenched in sweat and he could hardly talk he was so out of breath. I was after taking my leave of him when the fiddler struck up "St. Patrick's Day in the Morning."

"Now Bridget, you shan't sit this one out!" he says, and so he was pulling me through another one. Down the line from us trotted your Granda with the old lady, making her flush pink with all of his *plamas* - sweet talk - about how she was "the prettiest belle in the ballroom," to use his own words. Behind them was Hannah. All aglow she was, for she'd managed to coax Dr. Turner into the set.

After all that I was wanting to sit down with a glass of raspberry shrub, but Granda insisted that we dance a set, so 'twas a half hour later when I at last stole away to a seat. Me feet were heavy as lead and I couldn't coax them to shift if I'd wanted them to, but Granda kept on dancing with old Mrs. Brewster and had a turn with Hannah before the fiddler ended his set.

I tell you, the guests were having such a good time they seemed not to notice that the music had stopped, but sure they noticed Tirza as she made her grand entrance. Her gown was of periwinkle blue, the same color as her eyes. She wore brass beads that shimmered like gold, and her hair was crowned with more beads and two bright pink plumes, which was all the fashion in those days. Her fan was made of turkey feathers that she'd sewn together herself, and she swept it gracefully by her side as she sallied around that ballroom.

Tirza was enjoying the attention, and the young bucks were after begging her to dance with them, but she caught the eye of a handsome golden-haired stranger who looked at her from across the room as if she were the first woman he had ever laid eyes upon. He squirmed through the crowd and took her by the hand, just as the music was starting up again. 'Twas a glorious sight to see; the way the two of them danced! Like fairies they were, seeming to float on the air. Never had I seen such graceful dancing!

Sure I will never forget that night when Tirza Brewster met Joshua Spencer. He had come up from Georgia to visit some relations in Worcester, but they were soon forgotten, for the enchantment came over him as soon as he spotted Tirza! Later she claimed that he "came to the question" on the night they met.

Still, "the course of true love never runs smooth," as they say. She came to me one day all teary-eyed. "Oh Bridget, I am just devastated! We will be living in Atlanta, near Mr. Spencer's law office, for he cannot stay away from his practice for long. We want to be married at Thanksgiving but Father and Mother are being terrible about it, just because he comes from the South and his father owns three slaves. We have no plans to own any, so they should be happy for us and agree to the wedding. Do you think we should wait until Father gives his approval or should we go to Georgia and be married there instead?"

"'Tisn't me place to tell you what I think," I says to her. What I really thought was that she was too much of a flirt to be settling down! And Joshua Spencer was no bargain, in me own mind. True he was handsome and clever as a crow, but he was a snob. One day after we were done making butter Hannah and Tirza wanted tea, and we were all down in the old sitting room, drinking it when Mr. Spencer showed up unexpectedly.

Sure Tirza was all excited to see him, and Hannah was as gracious as usual. You'd never know she didn't much care for him. "Oh do sit down, Mr. Spencer," she says to him. "We have plenty of tea. You can sit next to Bridget here."

Well by the look on his face, you'd think she told him to sit next to a skunk!

"Really, do you make it a habit of taking tea with the servants?" he asks.

Now Hannah was after shaking with outrage, she was. "Bridget is not a servant, Mr. Spencer," she tells him. "She is hired help but we all share in the work, and she deserves a cup of tea as well as we do. We do pride ourselves here in Massachusetts, sir, on being an egalitarian society - albeit an imperfect one. Besides, we enjoy her company. Do we not, Tirza?"

But I could see that Tirza was betwixt and between defending me and pleasing her suitor. All she could do was stammer. "W-well, actually it was our Grandmother who said that the - ah, help should eat with us and - and it really is an old country custom. I suppose it is not *la mode* in the cities where they are so much more advanced socially -"

I'd had enough of her blithering. "'Tis alright Miss Tirza. I'm just after leavin', anyway. The children will be comin' home from school directly."

As soon's I stepped out of the room I heard Mr. Spencer speak to Tirza. "You must understand, my love, that it just isn't done that way in Atlanta. Why the Irish are hardly better than the blacks! They need to know their place." Well I knew of a place for Mr. Spencer and 'twould be a lot hotter than Atlanta!

I don't think the Brewsters ever took to Joshua Spencer that much. They were always saying that slavery was an abomination - I think that was the word - so 'twas was hard for them to accept that Tirza was after marrying a man who had grown up with it. They were dead set against anyone owning slaves and could not bear to think that their daughter's future in-laws did. Matilda also carried on a bit about her "baby girl" going so far away. 'Twas hard enough that her oldest son William had gone west years ago and rarely wrote home to say how he was getting on.

Eliphet Brewster objected to Tirza's marrying because he thought she was too young. "She only just turned twenty-one," he told Mr. Spencer. (It's always been a wonder to me how the Yankee ladies wait until they are in their mid-twenties before they wed. As Granda once suggested "Perhaps that accounts for their dour expressions!") But age was not a problem for Tirza's intended. It seems that like the Irish, the Southern ladies wed at an earlier age than their Yankee cousins, and Tirza was on the verge of spinsterhood if you could believe Mr. Spencer. So the Brewsters gave their blessing after all and Tirza and her beloved were married in the best parlor one blustery Thanksgiving night, after the piles of food were demolished and the men could button up their waistcoats again. There was no music, no dancing, no procession, and not much in the way of socializing afterwards. A few words in front of the Justice of the Peace, a wine toast and bite of cake, and the couple was off on their wedding trip. They planned to travel around the South, visiting Mr. Spencer's relations before setting down in Georgia. I don't think they were down there for one month before Tirza was after writing sorrowful letters home about how dull it was there and how she missed her old life in the North.

Bridget's Home

My grandmother and grandfather continued to live and work at the Brewster farm from 1830 until 1835. My Uncle Mike was born there in 1833, two years after my Uncle Pat. All of the children attended the district school, which like our common schools nowadays, was free for all children, even the Catholic ones.

Our Michael was a brawny lad with a good set of lungs on him right from the start. What with all the cryin', Matilda Brewster often complained that we were not only keeping HER awake, but old Mr. Brewster as well, and he was after suffering from a stomach ailment. He seemed to be having dyspepsia quite a lot in those days, until come one morning he couldn't get out of bed for the suffering. Sure Dr. Brigham did all the usual treatments of purging and bleeding and administering doses of calomel, but the old man grew so weak and thin that it seemed he would soon disappear into the bed pillows. The doctor decided to forgo the calomel and purging in favor of using laudanum to ease the pain. There was nothing else to do. When the end finally came it seemed a blessing, for old Mr. Brewster suffered horribly, God rest his soul.

Eliphet Brewster took over the farm, and now Matilda was the lady of the house, even though old Mrs. Brewster was still alive. By the terms of the will, the widow inherited one half of the house, but Matilda made it quite clear who was in charge. For one thing, unlike in the old man's time, she did not want the hired help sitting at the table with the family for meals. We had to eat in the kitchen after they had their fill, and on some days there was slim pickings by the time the Brewsters were done with their dinner.

The old lady was after taking to her room, and who could blame her? There was Matilda sashaying about with her two daughters, giving out orders just because she could. How she put me in mind of me sister Eileen! Now instead of doing just the dairying she had me doing many other household tasks, and I had to be quick about it or she would threaten to have her husband dock me wages. At four dollars a month I couldn't afford any wage docking. I preferred working alongside Hannah Brewster. Sure she would never pass for a beauty, seeing as she was buck-toothed and droopy-eyed, but she was of a kindly disposition towards me. Quite a talker she was, too. She never spoke a sentence without at least ten words in them, and half of those large enough to be three in one! 'Twas because she loved learning, you see. She was always after reading up on something. Well one day as we were going over her mother's list of instructions, Miss Hannah noticed that I was holding the paper upside down.

"Do you not know how to read, Bridget?" she asks me.

So the truth was out! I had always been ashamed of me own ignorance, but couldn't see as to how I could fix that.

"Sure, Miss Hannah. I can read and write some in the Irish, but not in the English. We were never allowed much in the way of schoolin'."

"Well here in New England we take pride in our literacy," she says to me. "Henceforth, Bridget, you are to come to me every evening and I will instruct you in how to read and write in English."

She turned out to be a good teacher, and while I would never be a profligate - em, prolific reader, in six months' time I could at least read notices and write me own name, and after a while I could read the Missal and the Boston Pilot, too. I often asked her to write down all of the silver dollar words she used so I could try them out from time to time, just to sound more educated. So one day Hannah put a book into me hand - a very heavy book. 'Twas a good half a ton of pages, I was thinking.

"Here, Bridget," she says. "You may borrow this from me. This will help you to learn new words, far more than I can teach you. Noah Webster's dictionary defines over 10,000 words!"

Ten Thousand! Sure it was too much to pour into me brain, the knowledge that there were so many words to learn! But Miss Hannah said I mustn't worry about knowing all of them but to try to learn the ones I was curious about and that should be enough.

In fact, my grandmother has two marbled copybooks filled with words, their pronunciations, and their meanings that Hannah Brewster had written down for her. She also had several sentences that were used by Miss Brewster. Apparently she had memorized them, for it was those phrases that she recollected and utilized in our interviews.

'Twasn't Hannah who was in charge of the dairy but her mother, and as time went on and the markets were less profitable she became a harder task mistress. Me duties expanded to include not only some cooking but the laundry besides. The work was heavy on me back, and since I was carrying another child, I could barely lift the heavy clothesbasket up and down the stairs.

About six months after old Mr. Brewster had passed on, the Widow Brewster had me in for tea one afternoon, and she told me she was worried for me health.

She commenced to scold me, so. "You should not be doing that type of labor in your situation, Bridget."

I says to her, "Yes ma'am, but try tellin' that to your daughter-in-law. Why, she'd dock me wages faster than a wren would fly on St. Stephen's Day!"

I saw her wince at that remark. She disapproved of any references to the saints. She said it was a "heathen" thing to do. Old Mrs. Brewster told me that I mustn't mind Matilda because she meant well.

I wanted to believe that but I had me doubts.

A week or two after me talk with the widow, I was delivered of a baby girl. Oh, she was a beauty, she was! Eyes blue as the sky, skin as white as milk and cheeks fair as the palest pink rose she had, and that babe was blessed with a full head of raven black hair that would fall into curls about her face. We called her Rosaleen, the Irish for "little Rose." Granda said she reminded him of that song, "The Dark Rosaleen." Of all of the children, our little Rose cried the least and smiled the most, and 'twas clear to see that she had bewitched her father's heart.

But not Matilda Brewster's! Far from it! Even though Rosaleen was not a great one to cry a lot, any show of tears was too much for the she-devil's sensibilities.

"All we need is another mouth to feed!" Matilda says to your Granda. She even convinced Eliphet to deduct twenty-five cents from our wages every week to go towards room and board for a child who was no bigger than one of their pumpkins!

The baby was barely creeping when I was asked to clean the Widow Brewster's rooms one day.

When I saw her, I tell you, me heart nearly stood still. The poor old lady was laying on her sofa still dressed in her nightclothes, though 'twas nearly noon. Her eyes were deeply circled and she was pale as paper.

"Ma'am, is it poorly you're after feelin' today?" I asks.

"Yes, Bridget, I have no idea of what has come over me. I felt so weak I had to sit down and I cannot even make it to my bed." Indeed, she could barely speak, never mind move.

"Here, let me help you," I tell her, "an' then I'll fetch Mr. Brewster."

We never made it to the sofa, for just as I slipped me arms about her she made a queer sound that held the hint of a *banshide's* wail in it, then exhaled a deep, raspy breath and died. You know, I think I cried more at her passing than her own son and daughter-in-law did. Oh, they were cold as clams at the funeral. Not one tear fell from their icy eyes, although Miss Hannah sobbed when they put the coffin in the ground.

Sure, there was more passion in the heated whispers and displays of bad temper going around the house a month after the funeral. 'Twas a warm June day but the air inside the Brewster home was frosty indeed. It all started that morning when Eliphet came home from the country store with a letter in his hand. I could see scarlet under his tanned face, and when he talked, the anger was after steaming out of his mouth.

"Read this, Matilda, and tell me if all those years of Christian teachings about the evil of slavery were for naught!" He handed the letter over to Mrs. Brewster and she read but two lines afore she burst into tears.

"How could she? And how could you have allowed her to marry that man and live among those sinful people?"

Mr. Brewster tried to point out to his wife that they both allowed Tirza to marry Mr. Spencer and go live in the South, all the while forgetting that 'twas their daughter's own decision to make - and sure that spoiled brat would have eloped if her parents had not given the match their blessing!

Matilda commenced to declaring that no matter what they had let Tirza get away with before, 'twas now their moral obligation to prevent THAT from happening. I wouldn't find out what THAT was for a while yet.

A few weeks after the letter's unwelcome arrival, there was more excitement in the house. Tirza arrived one day in a stagecoach, looking as if she'd been crying for weeks. She could have woke up the dead what with all of her wailing Matilda asked her, "Whatever were you thinking, allowing slavery into your household, after all that you have been taught?"

Tirza was after sobbing so hard her tears drenched her dotted Swiss bodice.

"But Mother, it is the Southern way of life, and Mr. Spencer knows no other. Besides, with my confinement approaching, I need the help of an experienced woman."

But Matilda Brewster would not hear any excuses.

"Experience! Yes, the experience of the lash! Have you forgotten that the unfortunate woman would have no choice and no remuneration for her work? Tirza, have you forgotten everything that you were taught?"

And didn't that squeeze more water out of the girl's eyes! I thought she would drown in her own tears, but Eliphet came into the room and she ran into his arms. He told Matilda to hush.

"She is home now and safe from evil. Dr. Brigham will attend to her."

'Twas Hannah who told me the rest of the story. It seems that once Tirza got down South and got accustomed to the place, she no longer had strong feelings against slavery. Especially since it was so helpful to have servants who were at her beck and call and did not expect to drink tea at her table. So when she learned that a baby was on its way, she assured her mother that she would be well attended when her time came, for her "servant" would look after her.

'Twas that she wrote in the letter, and 'tis how Tirza ended up coming back home to have the baby. The Brewsters were not about to let their grandchild come into the world by the hands of a slave.

Sure, Matilda Brewster was happy to have her daughter back home for the delivery. Her conscience was clear – but her household arrangements were another matter. In a crowded house (despite its having twelve rooms), she had to find a quiet place for her daughter. "Your two brothers are here, and Aunt Silence has come down from Maine to stay with us. She is sharing Hannah's bed, and your brothers are in Grandmother's old chambers and -"

"Well," says Tirza, "that is easily remedied, Mother. Aunt Silence and Hannah will stay where they are and I will take Grandmother's chambers. The boys can sleep in the rooms above the barn."

"But Tirza," Matilda says to her, "the Culligans occupy the barn chambers."

Do you know what that Mrs. High Muckety-Muck said to Matilda about us? She says, "Well they can just move out! I need Grandmother's rooms, and so we have to put the boys above the barn. That is the only remedy. You will agree with me that the time has come for those Irish layabouts to leave and learn to fend for themselves anyway."

But Tirza was told by her mother to share her bed with the old aunt for the time being. When she protested that she needed more room Matilda told her, "Do stop fretting about it. Your father will arrange something."

So that evening, Matilda asked Granda and me to come to the parlor. When we walked into the room Eliphet was there, pacing back and forth. Without his hat, his forehead glowed like a star in contrast to his field - darkened face.

"Bridget, Paddy -" The younger Mr. Brewster never learned our real names. "Mrs. Brewster and I want you to know how much we appreciate your work here, especially all that you did for my parents in their last days. But our situation has changed now. Tirza needs to stay here until after her child is born, and so, much to my regret, we can no longer keep your family here. You must leave by October. Of course we still want you to work here, and I will inquire around town about possible rooms for you."

We had barely four months' time, and I wondered where we'd go. I told your Granda about me concerns when we returned to our rooms that night.

"You know, Moira," he says, "I'm after thinkin' of findin' a job with the railroad. They pay good wages an' we could live in the camps with our own kind."

I just wouldn't hear of it! "Not the camps! There are wild fightin' gangs there from Kerry and Wexford an' there's filth and disease! I don't want the children to be gettin' sick or learnin' the ways of the Ribbon Boys." Granda insisted 'twas the best choice, but he knew I wasn't enthused about the scheme. No matter - he tried to reassure me that all would be well. "We have healthy children. They'll be fine, I'm after thinkin'."

Oh, if we 'd only known!

Young Pat had started at the district school that summer. He'd been attending for only three weeks when he came home early one day. "I'm feelin' poorly, Ma 'am," he says.

I felt his forehead. 'Twas burning up with fever! "Go right to bed now. I'll be up as soon as I'm finished hangin' the laundry," I tells him.

A while later I looked in on him. His face was covered in red spots! Measles for sure! Jacob and Zeke Brewster were sent away to stay with an aunt in Boston, and Matilda ordered us to stay inside our rooms. Doctor Brigham was sent for when our other wee ones began to bloom with spots.

But the Culligans are a rugged lot. Sure, the children were right as rain in no time - except for Rosaleen. She cried day and night, and nothing would comfort her. Her rosebud lips were cracked from fever, and she now weighed less than a feather. We were after trying everything, that the doctor suggested, and we prayed to the Blessed Mother day and night, but one rainy July morning, our little Rose sighed - 'twas like an angel's whisper - and then she died in Granda's arms.

Mr. Brewster paid for the burial and the services of Fr. Fitton, our priest. She was buried in Worcester. Quentin O'Toole provided the small headstone. I told your Granda that 'twas just as well Worcester was too far for me to walk to very often, for I hated to visit the grave. 'Twas unbearable; the sight of that rock, binding our baby to the earth!

At least I could take comfort in me rosary, but Granda wouldn't pray. "Who's even listenin' up there?" he'd ask. I'd tell him not to blame God.

Well, he'd say, "Can ye think of anyone better to blame? Where was He when I asked Him to spare our Rosaleen? He's just too busy to care about the likes of us, so from now on, I'll be too busy to care for Himself!"

He'd lost his faith but he found the bottle. When the work of the day was done, he'd have a glass of rum. Or two. 'Twasn't too long before he was after taking it in the day as well as the night. I lived in fear that the Brewsters would smell the drink on him. Eliphet Brewster was President of two Temperance Societies, and Matilda was a force in the Ladies' Temperance Organization. "Ardent spirits" were only to be drunk in moderation, and Granda wasn't moderate.

One night, I tried to talk some sense into the man.

"Please, machree, don't have another glass! What if Mr. Brewster sees you?"

But being so stubborn he wouldn't listen. "What indeed! He has seven grown children and soon a grandchild besides. He should have me sorrows," he says. I tell him, "I'm sure there'll be more sorrow for us if you lose your job."

As I said, your Granda was a thick-headed man. "I'm not after losing this job. I quit."

I couldn't believe he said that.

"Quit! Are ye out of your mind? Don't tell me you're after goin' to work on the railroad!"

"I am," he says. "I start in two days' time, and I've found a place for us to live, too."

Now how could I talk him out of it?

"In the shantytowns, you mean? You know how I feel about that! The children..."

He wouldn't let me finish. "The children will be fine there, but if I stay here, sure I'll go mad. Everywhere I go in this house, I'm reminded of her. I dream of her every night and sometimes I swear I can hear her cries. I have to get away from here, mavourneen. So, we'll be leaving tomorrow, and there s no arguin' with me. I have decided!" There was a new hardness in both his voice and in his eyes that made me shudder.

What was there to do, so? There was no use in trying to change his mind. He was too determined to go. So the next day we packed up our few belongings and took leave of the Brewsters. Eliphet shook Granda's hand.

"Remember, Paddy, it would please me to give you a letter of reference anytime," he says. Matilda merely asked if we'd swept out our rooms.

We were almost out of the gate when Hannah Brewster ran up to us. "Wait, Bridget!" she calls to me. The horse-faced girl was smiling, which only made her bucked teeth look bigger. She held out an ash-splint basket.

"Here, this is for you, Bridget." In it were some cheese, apples, gingerbread, a copybook and pencil, and large leather-bound volume that read: "A Dictionary of the English Language by Noah Webster." The gifts were covered by Old Mrs. Brewster's paisley shawl.

I took the basket from her hands.

"'Tis very kind of you, Miss Hannah," I says. But when I tried to give her back the shawl, she wouldn't take it!

"No, it is for you," she says. "Grandmother had given it to me but I am sure she would have liked for you to have it. She was very fond of you, Bridget."

She smiled at me again. She wasn't all that homely, I was thinking. I was after thanking her properly but I barely got out the words, for the tears were cluttering up me throat.

So Hannah whispers in me ear. "Please, do not hesitate to call upon me if ever you need some assistance, promise?"

I promised, but before I could say anything else to her, Granda took me arm and we headed for Green Street and the railroad.

Chapter IV.

The Paddy Shacks

At the sight of the paddy camps, me heart sickened. It was far worse than I imagined. The shacks were smaller than the huts in Ireland, and more poorly constructed. Indeed, constructed would be too generous a word for the gap-riddled hellholes where grimy children stared out of small glassless windows at each new arrival, while their mothers smoked clay pipes and tried to ignore the muddied road littered with filth. At that time of day, only a couple of men were to be seen. One had a mangled arm and the other staggered towards a reekin' privy, but the drink in him made it a wasted trip.

There was an empty "house," so-called, near the end of the road. "This is it," says Granda. "It won't be bad once you put yer hand to fixin' it up so."

Not a hand but a miracle was needed! The inside was dark and dank and smaller than what we had left in Ireland. There were cracks in the wooden siding that were large enough to fit a child's head through them. The floor was the same. Ragged bits of dried grass poked up from between the floorboards, and in the darker corners of the room mushrooms were growing and thriving. Outside, rats nosed around the steps, perhaps hoping that the new inhabitants would have a few crumbs to offer them. The sight of them made me shudder. I prayed we wouldn't have to stay there for long.

But Granda whispers in me ear. "Don't worry. We'll get out of here as soon as I've saved enough for us to rent a house. You'll see, mavourneen."

He left us there to settle in whilst he went in search of firewood to use in a wooden barrel. That served as both a chimney and a heat stove. As it turned out, there wasn't much wood to be had, and what was to be found was greener than clover.

Only a few days after we arrived there in Green Street, I feared for me life - and the children's as well. For there were Ribbon Men everywhere: wild gangs of young toughs who'd belonged to murderous secret societies back in the Old Country. There were rivalries between men of different counties; with the Kerrymen fighting with the Wexford men who fought with the Cavan men... sure 'twas a terrible situation, there! What with all the brawling and drinking and thievery going on, I wouldn't let the children out alone.

The only good thing that I can say about living in a shantytown is that it was nice to hear the Irish spoken again and to have neighbors to laugh with, pray with, and mind each other's children. And Granda seemed to be happy in his work. Sure his back ached of an evening but he was proud to put the cash in me hand on payday. At first anyway.

A man's wages on the railroad in those days was part cash and part rum. Yankee workers were given a pint of the brown poison a day in order to slake their thirst, and many a man took more than a passing liking to it. Your Granda was one of those men. Once again, he started to have a drink or two in the evening after work. He stayed at the shebeen (the barroom) later and later every night. By wintertime he'd have a jar of rum before the workday began. When Granda finally come home, he'd be so full of the drink he wouldn't want to eat the food set before him. Just as well, too. A year after we moved to the camps, he was spending so much on rum there was hardly a penny left over for our daily bread. Since coming to America our bellies never knew the pangs of hunger, but now our larder would oft-times yield up only some salt pork and corn meal, which I never got around to liking. The children were getting thin, 'specially the boys. But 'twasn't just the food we were lacking. The following winter, all four of the children went to school without warm clothes and decent shoes. Indeed, the day came when there was nary a shoe to be had between us.

Something had to be done. At first, I tried to get Granda to stop drinking. Sure he was near crazy without the drink as he was crazy from it! He was after driving me mad as well.

'Twas one evening I was after throwing out the rum bottle. I thought he was asleep, but I was mistaken. He leapt up from the bed and grabbed the bottle away from me so violently that it broke, cutting his hand. His eyes blazed with anger as he clamped his bleeding hand hard on me arm. "What are ye after doin', yer streely-haired crone? Think ye can keep me comfort from me, do ye?" I was afraid he would hit me, though he had never done so before. He didn't that night, either, but I was now desperate to get him away from the drink.

I knew better than to hide it after that, so I next tried to divert him. "Look," I says to him one day, "I have some tea from O'Toole's. Why don't you have a cup with me? It'll warm you more than rum."

"An' what would you be knowin' about that, Woman? Save your tongue for somethin' that makes sense, and shut yer gob about what a hard workin' man chooses to drink."

Well, if he wouldn't stop drinking, I thought, at least I could keep him home in the evening instead of staying out at the bar rooms.

"Please, could you stay home with me tonight? 'Tis so lonesome here after the children go to bed."

But he would speak to me so with a voice full of sorrow. "An' haven't I felt lonesome, too, ever since... ever since she was taken away? How can I stay here and hear the sounds of the other children, when one is missin' amongst us? Sure me heart aches as well as me back, an' the rum helps them both."

I hate to say it, but the drink, - the Irish Curse - was turning him into a Paddy. A slack-jawed, rusty-eyed, reeking sketch of a man whose drunkenness gave reason for the Yankees to sneeringly forget that he once had real dreams and a real name. 'Twas as if Barnard Culligan had gone to the grave with his daughter and had been replaced by a rum-addled changeling. I no longer knew the man. He'd become a Paddy to me and stayed a Paddy to me for so many years that for a long while I forgot that he was ever anyone else.

But I refused to be part of it all: the camps, the missed days at work, the stench of sickness, the poverty... It was time to take some action or we would never get out of it all.

So one warm spring Saturday I left Siobhan and Kathleen in charge of the boys and I walked down to see the railroad boss. I had to time it just right - not early enough for Granda to see me, but not so late that the office would be closed for the day.

The clock struck twelve. I had but a few minutes until Granda would be claiming his wages. The boss, Mr. Peavey, was still in his office.

"Yes?" He looked up from the paper he was reading.

"What do you want? Not a position, is it? I already have a housekeeper."

"Oh no, sir. I'm not here for a job. I'm after wantin' to ask you somethin'," I says.

"Well, what is it then?" he asks.

"'Tis help. Me husband is Barnard Culligan."

"And..?"

"And I'm wonderin' if could you give me his pay packet every week. So I can keep him from spendin' it on the drink," I explains.

Mr. Peavey rubbed his eyes, so. They were wreathed in dark circles. "D----ed Irish," he mutters. But then he spoke in a gentler voice than I would have imagined could come out of such a cross-looking man,

"I understand," he says to me. "But perhaps it would be better if I only gave you half his wages. I can tell him we are cutting back on his pay. As long as he has the money for rum, he will not miss the rest. You Irish are all alike that way. I never touch the bottle, of course. Pity your husband can not do the same."

I bit me tongue. "Thank you sir for your kindness, sir. May God an' Mary bless you."

"Yes, well-" he got up and he showed me the door. "Come by at this time every Saturday, and I will instruct my clerk to give you the wage packet," he says. "We shall start next week. Now you should best hurry along before he sees you here."

Now that I had half of Granda's money, I used most of it to pay bills and buy shoes for the children and copybooks for writing down me words, but I'd also put a little by every week into an old redware jar. I had to be cute about it. Sure if he found the money he'd drink it up. I tried to hide it near the privy, but I was afraid one of the children - or worse, a drunkard - might stumble across it. Finally I thought to ask Mr. O'Toole what I should do with it, and he told me to put it into a savings account.

I didn't know what he was talking about. "But I don't know how to keep accounts."

So Mr. O'Toole explained to me about banks. Most of them were for the well-to-do, he said, but now there was a new kind of bank that let women put in a little bit of money each week and it would turn into more money. I still didn't understand it, so he took me to the Worcester Savings Bank and explained to the banker that I wanted to open an account.

I was afraid to hand the money over to the banker. I thought he might never give it back! He had a grasping look about him: pinched cheeks and squinty eyes. But Quentin O'Toole assured me that it would be fine. "Don't you worry, Mrs. Culligan. The bankers will keep your money safe, they will. 'Tis good for business, after all!"

And he was right. Each week I would deposit a few cents into the account and after a year or two it started to add up. I was wondering one day how long it would take for me to save up enough to rent a farm, when Tighe Conlin - he was one of our neighbors and a good man, at that - came running to our door, panting for lack of breath.

"Tighe! What are you doin out of work this time of day?"

But me heart was already tightening, even before he told me.

"'Tis Mr. Culligan, Ma'am. There's been an accident," he says.

Railroad work is one of the most dangerous jobs a man can do. Sometimes, they have to blast dynamite into rocks and they end up blowing themselves up instead. Other men might fall through a trestle and die; or at best break a limb. The railroad workers often died young, or else they were so maimed that they might as well be dead, for all the support they could give their families. Sure I recollect Joshua Spencer once telling Tirza Brewster that in the South there is many an opportunity for an Irishman to find a job on the railroads, since the slave owners didn't want to lose their "investments."

"After all, a slave might be worth $1500. Now really, how much worth is there to a Paddy's life?"

I was always grateful that Granda was a digger, preparing the way for the men to lay the tracks. It seemed to be a lot safer job than many of the others on the railroad.

I would soon find out how wrong I'd been.

"Is he..?" I couldn't bear to ask the question.

"No, Mrs. Culligan. He is still alive." Tighe tried to sound reassuring, but how could I be assured of anything, knowing the dangers Granda faced?

"Is he - is he badly hurt?" I could barely get the words out of me mouth, it was that dry from fear.

"Well, not exactly hurt." he says.

"Where is he then?" I asks.

"In the Worcester Lunatic Asylum," says Tighe.

The Lunatic Asylum! I felt me mouth turn dry as chalk.

"How?" I asks, after catching me breath.

So Tighe told me how it all came about. It had been very hot that day. The July sun bore down on the men's flesh, burning them like meat on a spit. Granda and the other men wore hats to protect their fair skin from the sun's hateful rays, but on that day some important men and ladies were to visit the site. Mr. Peavey told the men to remove their hats until the visitors left. The guests stayed but a minute, since the ladies were feeling uncomfortable in the heat. But the workers had to stay on the job. There was nary a shady tree and it was a long time 'til the dinner bell. Granda waited until the Distinguished Personages left, and then he put on his hat again.

An hour later Mr. Peavey came by and knocked it off Granda's head.

"I said to take off your hat, Culligan," he says.

"I did, sir," says Granda.

"Liar!" Mr. Peavey says. "It is still on your thick Irish head."

According to Tighe, Granda then put down his shovel, which undoubtedly rose up the anger in his boss.

"Sir, I did take off me hat for the guests, but the sun is so hot I put it back on to prevent me head from burnin' up."

But for Mr. Peavey there was no excuse for disobeying his orders and even less of a reason to contradict his words.

"Listen, Paddy, when I tell you to take off your hat, you leave it off until I tell you to put it back on, now do you understand?"

"Yes sir," says Granda. The boss walked away still holding the hat. Even when everyone else was allowed to cover his head, Granda still had to work bareheaded.

'Twas almost 'til noon that he was hatless in that unforgiving sun. Sweat poured down his face and into his eyes, blinding him. By dinnertime, he was staggering about and sputtering gibberish like a mad man. 'Twas then that Peavey asked Tighe to take Granda to the Worcester Lunatic Asylum.

Only 'twasn't insanity he was after suffering from but heat stroke.

Once committed, 'tisn't an easy thing to be released from the lunatic asylum. The very next day Quentin O'Toole took me down to visit Granda. I had to squeeze me eyes shut to hold back the tears. The place reeked of urine and sickness. 'Twas like being on the immigrant ship all over again. Granda was in a small cell that had iron bars on the one window. His hair was unkempt and he was wearing only his shirt. From all around the ward could be heard screaming that was far worse than the wailing of ten *bansidhes*.

Instead of embracing me Granda grabbed on to me arm so tight I thought the muscles would pop out of me skin. "You have to get me out of here, mavourneen, or sure I'll be as mad as the rest of them."

Mr. O'Toole promised to take up Granda's case with the authorities, but his pleading on Granda's behalf failed. The police would not listen to Quentin O'Toole's request for Paddy Culligan's release. As well-to-do as he might be in Worcester, Quentin O'Toole was still a lowly Irishman to them.

So next I went to see Fr. Fitton. He was an important priest in Worcester, well respected by many of the Protestant ministers as well as by our own people. Father went to many people trying to secure Granda's freedom, but finally he told me the sad news.

"I am very sorry Mrs. Culligan, but they refuse to release him; not even to my custody."

What was I to do? Four children to feed, and not a penny coming in! Besides the lack of food, the winter would be coming and we had no money for firewood. By October, we were shivering all through the night and for most of the day as the winds sailed through the cracks in the walls. 'Twas a desperate situation, indeed.

Siobhan and Kate were now eleven. They found work minding the little ones for Mrs. O'Toole, and their modest wages helped a little. And sure Quentin O'Toole extended us credit at his store. But the day came when Mr. Peavey himself came to the door.

"Mrs. Culligan, since your husband is unable to continue in his employment with the railroad, I must ask you to vacate these premises," he says to me.

You can imagine the hopeless feeling that came over me.

"But I have no job. No place to go," I says. I tried to make him understand our predicament, but he wasn't really listening.

"I am sorry," he says (though there was no sorrow in his tone). "But you must realize that I have a lot of workers in need of shelter."

Sure I could understand his reasoning but it didn't make it any easier. Even if I hated the shanty where we'd been living for all those years, didn't I hate even more the idea of not having a roof over our heads?

As he did so many times before, Quentin O'Toole came to our rescue.

"I have two vacant rooms above my shop," he says. "You can stay there and do laundry for my other tenants as a way to pay the rent. Mind you, you would be doing me a favor if you take them. 'Tis good for business, after all. Unlet rooms invite vandals."

I was sorely grateful to the man. The rooms were small but clean, and since the tenants were all Irish - many just come over - the children and I felt right at home. Mike and Pat attended Mrs. O'Toole's school for Catholic children, and the boys also earned money helping out in the store. And didn't I have plenty of laundry work to do! For it seemed as if new tenants were arriving daily.

We were all settled down into our new life - until a dirty, bristly-faced man burst into the back door of the shop one night.

He was a sight to behold and a stench to the nostrils. His long hair was greasy and matted, and his gray-speckled beard tripped down onto his dirt-encrusted shirt. With the hair and the beard and the fierce look about him, he might have passed for a Biblical Prophet if he'd been of a saintlier disposition, but his clothes were full of holes rather than grace. He was singing at the top of his lungs and swigging a bottle of cheap rum.

> *It 's 'Pat do this an' Pat do that,'*
> *Without a stockin' or cravat,*
> *An' nothin' but an ol' straw hat...*

"Moira, mavourneen, I'm home at last!" Sure I knew that voice!

"Barnard Culligan!" Well now, I rushed over to him and fell into his arms, but he was reeking of spirits and I soon broke away from him.

"So they released you at last?" I asks.

"Release me! They didn't release me. I escaped!" When he said that, the pride made his chest puff out like a banty rooster's.

He stood before me, teetering back and forth from either the rum or from holding back the laughter; I couldn't be sure. I hoped it was a joke, 'though he'd not been disposed to making any since Rosaleen died.

"*Ramais* - nonsense!" I says. "How could you escape when they're after puttin' iron bars on all the windows and lockin' all the doors?"

He laughed at that and then reached over on his unsteady legs. He pulled me to him and whispered in me ear, 'though 'twas done so loudly he could be heard in Boston:

"I hid in the laundry basket!"

"Wha---? Did I hear that right? Laundry basket indeed!"

"Sure the man comes every Monday for the wash, an' I observed that he always came to me own cell next-to-last," he says. "So when his back was turned, I crawled into the basket an' hid under some dirty sheets. You should have heard him cuss, so! The basket must've weighed as much as a bullock!

"Weren't you afraid of gettin' caught?" I asks him.

"Woman, do you take me for a fool? Sure he caught me!"

I felt so wobbly I had to sit down. Me husband, escapin' from the lunatic asylum! By now, the children had gathered round us. I asked Siobhan to make us some tea and told Pat to fetch Mr. O'Toole.

"*Amadan*!" I says. "Amn't I the wife of a fool! By now, the man's probably gone to the police and they'll be after knockin' at our door. Sure you'll be locked up forever now, an' what will we do then?"

But the fool just laughed at me! "Don't worry so, mavourneen. The man was drunk when he came to fetch the laundry, an' once he left the asylum an' got into his cart he took out his bottle of rum an' got even drunker until he passed out in front of the gate. I was after thinkin' that come mornin' he wouldn't remember a thing, so I took the rest of his rum." Barnard Culligan was quite pleased with himself, he was! There was no reasoning with him. Well then Pat returned with Quentin O'Toole, who turned pale as a ghost when he saw Granda.

"He escaped," I explains.

"Not that I should blame him," says Mr. O'Toole.

"Come on, Barney, allow me to help you to your rooms and then we will think of what to do."

He and Pat brought your Granda upstairs. The man was dead weight, even though he'd lost a lot of flesh since he was locked up.

When I asked Mr. O'Toole what we should do, he only shrugged his shoulders.

"We can contact the asylum and tell them he is here. Or we can do nothing at all and hope he doesn't get caught by the police and sent back," he says.

We decided to do nothing at all.

Chapter V.
Cherryfield

Months went by. The police never came for Granda and eventually he got a job on the railroad again. This time he was working outside of Worcester with a different boss, a man named McCarthy, an Irishman. He and Granda got along well.

Then in 1840 my grandparents decided to find a new home. They had been living in the rooms above O'Toole's Dry Goods Store since the time Nana was evicted from the paddy shack in 1837.

I was still saving up money whenever I had a penny to pinch. I'd been doing laundry for several Yankee families who were all acquaintances of Mr. O'Toole. Mrs. O'Toole also found plenty of work for me. Good Christian that she was, the dear lady wanted to help out as many of her country women as she could, so nearly every day she'd knock at our door or stop me on the stairs with a request:

"Mary, the Glynns just had another baby. Do you think you can help me to launder clothes for them until Mrs. Glynn is feeling less poorly?" Or sometimes she'd ask me if I'd like to come in of an evening and help her to make new nappies and shifts for the Irish Ladies' Benevolent Society Clothing Bank. Other ladies, like Toby Boland's wife, would often be in attendance, and on those occasions sure I was painfully aware of me own faded frocks and the worn-out shoes that were holier than Mrs. O'Toole's prayers. Sure she was very devout and felt no opportunity should slip by without a word to Heaven, even when we were scrubbing clothes for the bachelor tenants. I prayed for the bachelor tenants, too - in the fervent hope that they'd get married and move away, leaving me with less dirty shirts to wash!

From the money I earned each week I would put a few cents into the bank account. It seemed that every month there were more tenants in need of clean clothes, for Quentin O'Toole was buying up properties faster than conies had kits! It led to a side business for the man: selling all of the old furnishings and other goods that the previous owners had left behind. As for meself, I was earning more money for the laundering, but it left me hands feeling raw from all of that scrubbing, and every time I looked at them, I was reminded of me own Mam and of how hard she'd worked. It made me miss her so.

Because of all the extra work I did for the O'Tooles, our rent was next to nothing, but the two small rooms were too cramped for the six of us. And 'twasn't just our flat that was crowded, mind you. Every month, more Irish were coming into Worcester and they all seemed to come to O'Toole's for a place to live. Sure Quentin O'Toole wouldn't turn anyone away, either for love or money. Giving them rooms, however small, was good for business after all!

But 'twasn't good for our own business. You couldn't go down the stairs or to the privy without having to walk behind a line of twenty other Irish tenants, it seemed. And then there was the matter of the kegs of rum that Mr. O'Toole sold in his store. Even though Mrs. O'Toole kept her husband at his word not to give or sell any to Barney Culligan, it still made me nervous having it so close by. When Granda finally started to talk of moving, no grass grew under me feet as I looked for places to rent.

As it turned out, only a few days after we decided to move who should come into O'Toole's Store but two familiar faces. Tirza Brewster Spencer wafted in looking quite the fashion plate in gray shot silk. She was accompanied by her sister Hannah, who was now Mrs. Abel Turner. Miss Hannah was also a mother, carrying one wee boy in her arms and clearly expecting another. Tirza was after busying herself with some plumes. Apparently, she lost one off of her bonnet in the railway car and she just had to have another immediately! She barely paid me any notice, but Hannah looked really happy to see me.

"Why look, Tirza! If it isn't our Bridget!"

"Who?" Tirza asks. Her voice had grown into a lazy drawl. She was carrying another child, too. She probably came back to New England to give birth at the Brewster's, I was thinking. I was also thinking that Tirza had forgotten I ever existed!

"Oh, yes. Good day, Bridget." She gave me a brief nod before continuing with her shopping, but Miss Hannah nearly drowned me with her flow of questions.

"How are you? What an unexpected pleasure to view your countenance again! Where are you living? I see that you still have Grandmother's shawl. It looks very becoming on you! Is Paddy still with the railroad? I heard that your two girls are working as hired help. How old are they now - eleven or twelve? I cannot remember. How long has it been since we last met?"

Sure that young woman could talk! I'd barely get around to answering one question when she'd put me through another! Finally, I got to ask about herself and so she told me that she and the doctor planned to leave the little house that they moved into the year they were married.

"You see, Bridget, my husband would like to have more room for his practice as well as for our growing family," she says. (And didn't she blush as if I couldn't see that her family was growing indeed)! "Dr. Turner has decided that instead of selling the cottage right away, he would let it to tenants as an investment."

So I asks her, "An' where is this house, if ye don't mind me askin'?"

"It is right outside of Worcester, in Cherryfield. It is but four miles to Father's farm. It is a lovely place, but rather small for us. Only three rooms and an attic, but the grounds are very amenable to one's agrarian proclivities! Dr. Turner planted some apple trees in the back and there is a barn where we keep the horse and carriage. It will grieve us to leave it, but he wants to remove us to the new home as soon as possible."

I hardly heard what she said after that. I just kept thinking about that house. How grand 'twould be to have our own land! Me head filled with visions of Granda at the plough, and meself picking the fruit off of those apple trees.

Well while I was daydreaming, Tirza had selected her plume and she was eager to quit the store. "Oh do stop chatting with Bridget and come along," she says to Hannah. She was attempting to whisper, but you'd have to be stone deaf not to hear what she was saying! "It is no use talking to her about that house, Hannah. How could those people possibly afford it? Stop putting any notions into Bridget's head about living beyond her means! Besides, I just might have Mr. Spencer purchase it from Dr. Turner. I could use a *pied-à-terre* when I come up North, even if it is rather close to the train station. I really cannot abide staying at the farm any longer. It is just too tiresome to hear Father go on and on about the immorality of slavery, without any consideration for Mr. Spencer's sensibilities!"

She gave me a smile as sweet as treacle. "Why Bridget, you could be my servant when I am summering here in Massachusetts! I am sure Father would have no objections, and it could improve your prospects for future employment, working for such a prominent family as ours."

Tirza didn't wait for a response from me but instead she took Hannah by the arm and pulled her towards the door. "Well come along, Sister. Mrs. Ward is expecting us for tea." Then she patted me hand as if I were her pet puppy." I will be sure to put in a word to Mr. Spencer about hiring you for my summer servant, Bridget."

A servant! No matter that Hannah or old Mrs. Brewster or even Mr. and Mrs. O'Toole called me "hired help" - 'twas a servant's work I'd been doing since I came to America. And I was tired. Tired of washing laundry and cleaning other people's houses while I lacked one of me own. 'Twas one thing to do it for the O'Tooles' lodgers and quite another to be doing it for a spoiled, childish belle who would begrudge me the wages that she could legally deny to a black woman. Enough!

Hannah said goodbye to me and was walking out after Tirza. 'Twas then that I remembered something she told me the day we left for the paddy camps: "Please do not hesitate to call upon me if you need anything." Well if I didn't need anything now, when would I ever? So I called out to her.

"Em - Miss Hannah?"

She turned around. "Yes, Bridget?" she asks.

"Em - how much would Mr. Turner be askin' for rent?"

'Twas hard to understand her reply at first, for all of the five-dollar words she used. "I cannot say, for being a woman I am not privy to pecuniary matters. Dr. Turner says it is an exceptional property, but with the railroad now so close by, we cannot hope to realize our previous expectations as regards to monetary renumeration-"

Then she stopped talking and looked at me as if she hadn't ever seen me before.

Her eyes grew as large as an owl's. "Would you and Paddy be interested? Of course, I would have to ask Dr. Turner if he would..."

"Rent to Catholics?" I asks. "Why Miss Hannah, we can prove our worthiness, if that's what your husband's after worryin' about. We must rent your house! It's just what we need: fresh air and a chance to grow our own food! And sure we'll take as good care of it as we would a home we built ourselves. Dr. Turner needn't worry. Mr. O'Toole will vouch for us. And sure didn't your father once say he'd give Mr. Culligan and meself references whenever we needed them."

Now Hannah Brewster Turner started to laugh! Not a delicate, ladylike giggle had she, but a full-bodied guffaw.

"Bridget Culligan," she says, "you could sell wooden nutmegs! I shall have a word with Mr. Turner. I trust that he and Paddy will come to some agreement."

Two days later, I got word from Hannah Turner that she and the doctor would stop by at two o'clock that afternoon to show us the property. I told her that Granda was feeling "indisposed" and couldn't come along with me, though 'twas only because I hadn't told him about the farm yet. I didn't see the need to get him involved until I could see the place and pass judgment on it.

'Twas but five miles from O'Toole's to Cherryfield, but I felt as if I'd entered a different world. What a pretty little town! All of the houses and shops around the common were neat and white; their dooryards lined with quinces or rose bushes or boxwoods. The Turner's place was less than a mile from the village center, on a gently sloping hill that guarded the Cherryfield River. There were tall elm trees that shaded the driveway back then. Sure two of them were struck dead by lightening later on in the '50s, but on that day when I first laid eyes on the place, they were in their autumn glory.

Miss Hannah commenced to telling me about the virtues of the place. "It is a short walk to town," she says, "and the trees afford some privacy from all th' - the railway workers and..."

I knew she was embarrassed so I said it for her. "Their paddy shacks? An' don't I know a thing or two about those!" But I assured her that it made no difference what I'd be looking at if I could have such a place to call me own. True, the paddy camp and the railroad was encroaching on the western side of the land, but oh, the rest of it was lovely!

Geese gathered in the river, and a grey cat was stretched out on the grass, eyeing them with thoughts of dinner, no doubt. There were three large fields, unkempt for lack of use, but sure they could be put aright with a few crops. Oh what a Paradise it seemed! There was also an orchard of red apples ripe for the picking, some hazelnut trees, pastureland, and a red carriage house that Dr. Turner said could easily be made into a barn.

He thought he needed to convince me. "I have no time for farming, what with my practice and all, although we have a kitchen garden and we have grown hay for our horses. The land is perfect for a small farm, and I think you will find that the house is of an adequate size."

The house indeed was big enough for us. I loved the sunny kitchen with its great hearth, although it had been bricked up for Hannah's cook stove. There was also a bedchamber and the surgery, which could become our parlor, and the attic was large enough for all our children to sleep in.

And then there was that grand back porch! I could just see your Granda and me sitting out there of a summer evening, watching the stars shine above the river.

I had to have that house! 'Twould be the salvation of us all; I was convinced of it.

"Well what do you think, Bridget?" Dr. Turner asks me. He was a poker-faced man, but I could detect a shadow of a smile on his lips. "I beg your pardon for discussing monetary matters with you, but you may tell your husband that I will reduce the rent by half a dollar a month if he will keep the property in good repair."

So I tells him straight out that I wanted to rent it and if ever we had the means, I wouldn't say no to buying it.

"Perhaps you might someday," says the doctor. "My father-in-law, Mr. Brewster, lends money for small mortgages, but at present I intend only to let it." He said it would be hard to find good tenants for the property because now it is in what most people considered to be an "undesirable location." The doctor said we could rent it for $1.50 a month, and he gave his word that if the house and land were to be sold in the future we would be told about it first.

"Do you think your husband will accept those terms?" he asks. I assure him that he would.

Convincing Dr. Turner to let his property to us was the easy part. Now came the hard part: I had to convince Granda to go along with the scheme.

I waited 'til Samhain - Hallowe'en. Back in Connemara, we'd be carving the jack-o'-lanterns and laying out a feast for the dead. There would be straw-masked beggars threatening to play tricks upon their "betters" for refusing to give them food, and young girls would cast spells to find their true lovers. What grand times they were! Now many of our countrymen were observing the night as they did in the Old Country. The children were off with the O'Toole's grandchildren playing games of fate, for 'twas the custom on the eve of the old year that people looked ahead to the new.

And what better time so to bring up the subject of our removal to the Turners' home? Though I had to scrimp and beg for the ingredients, I baked an extra large pan of *barm brac*, the traditional Hallowe'en cake that just happened to be your Granda's favorite. Inside the cake I added not just coins or matches or buttons - the usual charms - but also a key that I'd borrowed from Mrs. O'Toole. And didn't I just have the confection coming right out of the bake kettle when he came through the door!

"An' what's this?" he asks. I could tell he was very pleased. He gave me a kiss on the forehead as I cut off an extra large slice for him.

I says, "Well, it bein' Samhain an' all, I'm thinkin' we should find out our fortunes for the New Year."

"Fortune is it?" he laughs. "I feel fortunate enough to have for me wife a woman who knows her way around the hearth. Yer a wise woman, Moira Culligan. Sure you know how to keep yer man home on a cold autumn night! Well, let's see what Fate has in store for us!"

So he bit into the cake and spat out the key. "What in the name of Heaven is this supposed to be?"

"I took it out of his hand. "Why 'tis a key! A rare charm, indeed!"

"Rare, is it?" he asks. "What does it mean, so?"

I knew that the word "rare" would pique his interest! He was getting beside himself, he was that curious.

"Well, Woman, are ye going to tell me what it means or aren't ye?"

I swallowed some cake and washed it down with tea, for me mouth was dry with nervousness. "Why, it means a change of residence." I tried to sound surprised.

"An' where might we be removin' to? We need to find a place we can afford first, and those are hard to come by! Sure we have a roof over our heads here in the meantime, an' that's more than ye can say for some. Em - cut me another slice, Moira."

So I gave him a slice in which I put not a key, but -

"A penny! Arrgh!" Granda spat out a coin.

"An don't we know 'tis a sure sign of good fortune," I says.

Now Granda seemed a bit suspicious. "Woman, what's this all supposed to mean?" he asks.

"Sure I'm after thinkin' it means we'll be removin' to a new home soon; perhaps a real house with a field an' a river running alongside it -" I was doing me best to make it seem like a grand idea, one that he'd come up with himself.

"An' where would we be findin' such a place like that around here?" he asks.

Now I was just waiting for Granda to pose that question, so I says in a tone as innocent as a nun's, "You know, I didn't have the chance to be tellin' ye, but whilst I was down in the shop recently, didn't I run into Mrs. Turner!"

"Who?" I was hoping he'd ask.

"Sure you don't mean to be tellin' me you forgot about the Brewster's daughters?"

"Not that silly lass who married the man from the South? I thought she went out to Georgia or some place," he says.

"You're after thinkin' of the younger one," I says. "I'm talkin' about the older one. You know, the homely one who gave us the basket of food an' me her grandmother's shawl?"

"*Sea*, of course I remember her." Granda laughed at the thought. "Poor woman! She was ugly as sin, she was."

I'm ashamed to say I laughed along with him. "Well, you remember how she married that Dr. Turner? "

He was after wiping the crumbs from his mouth. "I don't know if she did or she didn't. What business does she have at O'Toole's? Aren't there enough Protestant stores for her kind?"

Now 'twas the time. I took a deep, deep breath.

"Well now, it seems her sister was after needin' a plume for her bonnet an' whilst she was lookin' for one, Miss Hannah an' I got to talkin' an' she told me they were removin' into town so she was after askin' would Mr. O'Toole know anyone who might want to rent their house in Cherryfield. She said 'tis a lovely house. It has a barn an an orchard an' 'tisn't too far from the railroad tracks an' it's to be let at a reasonable rent." I tell you, I was hoping and praying that he couldn't hear me hard breathing. But he was barely listening.

"What of it? No matter what, the rent would still be too much for us, Moira. We're fine where we are for now, I tell you. Besides, how could we be affordin' the expense of a removal? We'd need to rent a cart and purchase furnishin's."

"Surely Quentin O'Toole would lend us his cart," I says. "But I suppose 'tis the truth you're after speakin', indeed. Why should we pay $1.50 a month for the rent when it could be easily let to a Yankee at two or three dollars a month - though Hannah Turner say 'tisn't somethin' most Yankees would want, it bein' so close to the railroad tracks."

"In other words, it bein' so close to the Irish workers?" he asks.

"Perhaps that as well," I says. "But they're after lookin' for good tenants, and Dr. Turner says he'll reduce the rate for the right people: responsible tenants who'll take care of the place."

But Granda was a hard nut to crack. "Well 'tis no business of ours what they do. We're not goin' to live there."

Now I had to be cute - clever, as you'd call it. So I says, "Hmmm. I suppose you're right. After all, why should they rent to the likes of us, when there are plenty of good Yankee Protestants in Worcester to let the place? Why didn't that other one, Tirza, say she might be after buyin' it for when she visits up North? She said that maybe she'd even hire me to be her servant - an' wouldn't it be grand if there was a job for you in it as well! Sure a steady job in another's house is better than dreamin' in vain for a home of our own."

I tell you, Granda slammed his fist down on the table so hard it shattered the cup of tea I'd set down. I tried to wipe it up but he brushed me hand away.

"I'd work for the devil before workin' for that spoiled brat! Besides, what's so foolish about wantin' our own home? Why shouldn't we get somethin' we want for a change? How many years have we been here now Moira? Fifteen, sixteen? Too many to count. An' what do we have to show for it? Nothin'! Why should I work like a dog for these Yankee bosses an' then be refused a chance to live with me family in decent quarters? I'll show that horse-faced woman an' her bone-settin' husband! I'll not only demand to rent it, I'll buy it out from under them someday! Sure it can't be that hard to save up the money."

"Indeed," says I. "Especially since you've been puttin' by part of your wages all these years."

He looked puzzled, he did, but he tried not to show it!

"Wages? Em- Sure! I've been so busy slavin' away all this time I forgot all about them! I did put some by, didn't I? *Sea*, of course I did! Now, you know I've never been good at figgerin', mavourneen. So how much money would ye be thinkin' I've saved? "

"I'm thinkin' there's enough to rent the place and perhaps even buy it someday like you said." Oh, I was cute!

"That much I put by, did I? Well, 'tis Turner that I'll be speakin' to about rentin' the place - but mind you, Woman, 'twill be only if I like the looks of it."

So it came to pass that barely month later, we packed up our things into Quentin O'Toole's cart and removed ourselves to our new home.

The house was painted white, which was the fashion in those days. There were the two rooms downstairs, besides the kitchen in the lean-to, and two freshly papered and painted chambers in the attic where Turner children had slept. There was a chimney in the center of the house that was built to support a large fireplace in the kitchen and smaller ones in the other rooms, just as you'd see in most old New England farmhouses then. Inside the kitchen was a soapstone sink and a hand pump, and outside a working well. Hannah told me that there were many flowers that grew amongst the herbs and plants in the kitchen garden, but since we moved in November and the ground was carpeted in dead leaves, 'twas hard to imagine anything growing there.

The Cherryfield River ran alongside the back of the house. In the years to come I would often fall asleep at night to the sound of the rushing water. On me lonesomest day I'd look out at the river and think about how it would go out to the sea, and that the sea's waves would kiss the coast of Ireland - and wouldn't the homesickness come over me! But from the first day that I laid me eyes on it, I knew I'd never want any other home but that snug farmhouse in Cherryfield.

Sure, many might call it an undesirable location. 'Twas very close to the railroad, after all. The trains passed by only twice a day at first, but as the railroad expanded in the '40s so did the schedule - and the noise. No matter, that. We had room to breathe, and farm, and grow...

Nana could not recollect the exact date that they moved to the farm, but my mother says it was in the winter of 1840–1841. It was during the following year after they moved to Cherryfield that my grandparents' last child, my Aunt Anna, was born.

'Twas when the twins and the two boys were nearly grown that our Anna was born. She was fair and plump and healthy from the start - thanks be to God and Mary! Anna was a miracle child; born after I turned forty. Old age was nearly upon me.

Baby Anna made me forget the aches in me joints and the gray in me hair. She was a joyful child to be sure. With those golden curls and deep blue eyes and her laugh that tinkled like sleigh bells - well, would you blame us for thinking she was given to us by the *sidhe* themselves? Sure she loved to dance in the fields and hide in the hay stacks, jumping out at Granda and the boys and nearly frightening them out of their wits! Of all of me children, Anna was the easiest to raise. For didn't she have two brothers and two sisters that were so taken with her that they were mad to raise her up themselves!

The child was not only a miracle, but a miracle maker, too. The very joy of her birth made Granda resolve to give up the drink for good. 'Tis true he had a few lapses, but when the temperance priest, Fr. Theobald Matthew, came to preach in

Worcester back in '48, Granda was one of a hundred men who took the pledge.

Now that he was freed from the Irish Curse, Granda turned his full attention to our farm. Sure, 'twasn't much of anything to start with. We had a few hens and grew some beans and potatoes that first year. After that first year Granda expanded the number of crops a bit more each spring, and I earned money from selling eggs as well as doing laundry jobs. Five years after we first arrived in Cherryfield, we had enough saved to make an offer on the house.

The timing couldn't have been better. The Turners had decided to move to the West. They wanted to take care of old business before they left, which included the selling of the Cherryfield farm. One day Dr. Turner came to see us.

Perhaps he was after planning to sell the place to a Yankee in hopes of a better price, because he told us he'd take no less than $150 for it. Granda was crushed when he heard that. Still, he was after trying to do his best to buy it.

"Sure I can't afford $150, sir. 'Tis more than I've been able to put by in all these years," he tells him. Indeed, we were after hoping we could get the farm for $100, and even that would be a sacrifice.

But Dr. Turner wasn't about to bargain. Instead, he tried to convince Granda to forget about Cherryfield altogether.

"Why struggle here in the East, Culligan? Go West! A man can make his fortune there."

"A fortune isn't for the likes of us, Dr. Turner," Granda says to him. "We'd be just as happy with your house an' the three acres it sets on if you will sell it to us for $100. An' wouldn't the sale of it suit yerself as well, for 'twould take a long time to find someone willin' to buy a place so close to the railroad tracks and the Irish workers for $150!"

"Very well," says the good doctor. "You have the better argument, I must admit. If you can secure the funds I shall have the contract drawn up."

"'Tis a deal, then?" asks Granda.

"Conditionally," says Dr. Turner. "We have come to a temporary arrangement, but if you do not have enough means, you will need to secure a mortgage. Ask my father-in-law if he will lend to you."

So they shook hands on it. Now Granda had to visit Mr. Brewster and try to borrow the money for the mortgage. I went with him and I tell you, 'twas a shock to see how old Mr. Brewster looked. His face was as white as his hair, and the wrinkles on it were not only evidence of the years spent outside in his fields. 'Twas Tirza and that wife of his that aged him, I was after thinking.

Hannah had already talked to her father, so he wasn't surprised to see us. Indeed, he shook Granda's hand as if they were old friends.

"My daughter told me that you want to purchase Dr. Turner's property." He was after smiling at Granda. He'd always liked Barnard Culligan and he told him that.

"I know that you and Bridget are industrious, honest people," he says. "I would be happy to lend you the necessary funds, at the usual rate of 6% and a five year term. Is that agreeable?"

Granda said it was very agreeable, indeed. Mr. Brewster drew up the papers and we left with the mortgage money. The very next day, we went to see Dr. Turner and gave him $100, and he handed over the deed. Hannah made tea and a pound cake to mark the occasion and we all celebrated our good fortune. Sure the Turners felt fortunate too, since our purchase of the farm was their last business endeavor before heading West.

"Well, Culligan," says Dr. Turner. "It affords me great pleasure to allow you to purchase my property. It is very heartening to know that there are people like you among the Irish. Hardworking, honest, temperate, willing to do your part - I cannot say the same for these new arrivals."

Indeed, there were many more Irish coming to Worcester then: people who were much poorer, dirtier, and sicker than the hearty men who'd arrived in the '20s and '30s. The poor famine-ridden souls were half-starved to death by the time they arrived here. These new Irish thronged the Boston ports and the Worcester streets, begging for food, for alms, for mercy. 'Twas hard to look into their eyes, so haunted they were with the memories of having been to hell and back.

The Yankees barely tolerated our presence when we first arrived, but they needed us to do the dirty work that had to be done in order to become a strong nation: building the canals and roads and railroads. As long as we did the work in the way the Yankee bosses ordered it, they were willing to overlook our queer tongue and strange customs.

But now the ships were arriving in Boston every day with the weakened victims of the Great Hunger. Some were dead upon arrival, while others died before they could even find a place to rest their skeletal heads, poor souls. Most of them knew no other job than scratching out a living on rocky, wet soil. For years their British landlords allowed them little else but potatoes for food, but when the crops were blighted the English government refused to help. After all, 'twould interfere with free trade. Better to kill a few hundred Irish peasants than to damage one business.

So the Irish tenants sold whatever they could, begged passage from relatives already come over, and huddled into the coffin ships, crowding together in small, airless holds and lying in their own filth and vomit; sharing lice and fleas and disease. And because they looked so ill and wretched when they arrived many people were afraid to look at them, much less hire them for work. By the time we saw them in Worcester they had lost some of their pallor after having a chance to bathe and wash their ragged clothes, but they were still weak and often as wild-eyed as madmen.

Soon the Yankees started to despise not only the new arrivals but also anyone who happened to be Irish. People who once nodded to us on the streets now looked the other way. Yankee children scowled at our own. Sometimes the native brats threw rocks at Irish children while their American parents turned their heads the other way. It was during that time when the notices in the newspapers started to crop up like weeds: "Help Wanted. Anyone but Irish." Those were the days when every Irishman was a Paddy, every Irish woman a Bridget, and their children gossoons.

The railroad bosses began to come down hard on any Irishman who worked the line, even those like Granda who had been there for over twenty years. One day he came home from work with a question.

"Do yer think we can buy some sheep? An' another cow?"

"Sure, if the price is right."

"It has to be! 'Tis time I left the job. Me joints are always achin,' an' anyway 'tisn't the same with all the newcomers. I'm after thinkin' I'd like to turn me hands to farmin' an' me back to the railroad."

By then we'd paid off the mortgage. We took the last bit of money from the bank to buy four sheep and a young cow from Mr. Brewster. He gave us more than a fair price. Now we were not only landowners, but farmers, too.

You'd think I'd have been content with all that. For didn't I have a temperate, hard-working husband, healthy children, a warm, neat home and a farm that could hold its own against any of the Yankee ones? But something was bothering me, gripping me with fear during the day and darkening me dreams at night.

'Twas this thought that robbed me of sleep: I was after wondering what had happened to me family. Did they die from starvation? Maybe they took sick from the diseases that riddled the land. Or were they still alive, trying to survive the horror of never-ending hunger? Perhaps some of them were lucky enough to get passage. But if they did, there was no telling that they'd come to Massachusetts. They could be anywhere in America, or in Canada, or somewhere else. If only I knew for certain...

When I first came to America, before Miss Hannah taught me, I had no reading or writing on me. Sure, I could write me name in the Irish. I'd learned that from me older brothers. They'd gone to a hedge school for a time. But 'twouldn't do for me to set pen to paper, so, and write a letter to the family back in Ireland. I still had a poor hand, and they'd have an even poorer time of reading in the English.

Well, now, Quentin O'Toole subscribed to the Boston Pilot, the Catholic newspaper. It had a column in it each week called "Missing Friends." You could write in and ask if anyone had seen or knew about your family or friends from back home. I sent in me name and asked for information on the relations of Moira (nee Sullivan) Culligan, and every week I'd search the paper in hopes that one of them would be looking for me, but there was never any news.

So one day I was thinking of all of these things and wondering if I should try to write a letter to the parish priest back in Ireland, Fr. Coyne. But would he be alive, even?

I was interrupted in the search for pen and paper by a knock at the door. I opened it and backed away from fright. Falling into the doorway was a tall, pale-faced, dark-haired man with the long-jawed look of Connemara folk about him.

"God save all here," he whispers. I hadn't heard the old blessing in many a year. Sure his homespun clothes were ragged and his face thin, but he didn't have the tortured look of the famine refugees. Yet like many who were finding their way to our house in those days, he asked me for food.

"Please, ma'am, I've walked all the way up from New York an' I haven't had a bite to eat in a couple of days."

"Come in, so, an' be welcome at our table," I says to him.

"God and Mary bless you," he says in return.

I cut a large wedge of cheese and put it on a plate with bread and butter and leftover ham. I set it down in front of him and he fell to it hungrily, pausing only to gulp the cider I handed to him.

I watched him eat and drink his fill and then I asks him, "Have you been over long? "

"Near six months," he says. "I came over from Galway."

Galway! I couldn't believe it! I says to him, "Why don't I come from there as well! What parish?"

"Spiddal," he answers.

When I heard that I nearly fell off the chair! "An' who might your people be? For amn't I from Knocknadough! I was Padraic Sullivan's fourth child. Have ye heard of him?"

And he laughed! "Sullivan! Me wife's mother was a Sullivan from Knocknadough, God rest her soul."

Now a chill crept over me. "An - which Sullivan was she?" It could be a cousin, after all. The name was common enough.

"Eileen was her name," he tells me. "She married a man named Padraic Nee many years ago, when his curragh had capsized an' he washed up ashore. Her brother and sister had taken him to their home in Knocknadough an' that's how they met. He lives, but she died tryin' to bring her last baby into the world. Sure 'twas really the hunger that killed her off."

Tears flooded me eyes, so that I was looking at the man as if he was under water. "Sure that was me own sister, Eileen. An' wasn't I the sister who brought Mr. Nee home!"

At that, me visitor says, "Sure now I remember now! You were the aunt me wife never met, the one who went off to Americay. You must be Aunt Moira!"

I'd never been called an aunt before. It sounded so queer. But not so odd as the fact that a near relation appears at me door on the very day I decided to inquire about me family.

The young man's name was Liam O'Shea. His family died during the Hunger, mostly of the black fever, he said, and his voice was choked with tears at the memory of it.

"Your own Mam and Da were gone many years before the crops failed," he tells me. "Two of your sisters are gone, too, but as to the others - not all of them died from the hunger. Some went to England, an' some went to Dublin." That was all that he knew about me family.

We talked for hours afterwards, in the Irish. He told me about Granda's Aunt Assumpta, still alive - though well into her eighth decade - and of how Cousin Corny still traveled about the countryside playing for food, or lately, playing for wakes. There were so many dying there that he had plenty of work. Eileen's husband, Padraic Nee (the one I'd taken for a dead man years ago) was ailing. He was living with his youngest daughter, Mary - named after me, as it turns out! Sure me sister's family had suffered in those black times. But one of their sons was studying to be a priest, and Eileen's daughter Caitlin was now Liam's own wife. She was back in Ireland, waiting patiently for her husband to send for her.

"'Tisn't as easy to earn the money as I thought 'twould be," he says. And didn't that remind me of our own hard times years ago! Like your Granda, Liam O'Shea took any job he could get. He'd been working at a coal mine in Pennsylvania 'til the workers struck, and then he'd been up to New York City in search of work. Now he had hopes of a good job in Boston, he told me. The lad was desperate to send passage money to his Caitlin - me niece.

I saw a chance to get to know me nephew better, so.

"Sure, why not stop with us here a few days an' rest yourself? We've plenty to eat, an' 'tis nice to see kin after all these years."

He wouldn't stay, though. "I'm grateful to you, but I must get along. I'm afraid if I tarry I'll lose the job. 'Tis for a bricklayin' firm in Boston. Good wages, I'm told."

But I wouldn't let me only kinsman in America just walk out of me life!

"Well, Liam O'Shea," says I. "Now that we've found each other, don't be a stranger here. Bring your bride to meet her Aunt Moira an' Uncle Barnard."

"An' don't I know she'll be wantin' to meet ye. Until we meet again, God go with you, Aunt Moira." His voice was rough with tears and I was feeling water in me own eyes.

"An' God an' Mary go with you an' me niece." How lovely it felt to say that!

I told Liam 'twas a pity he couldn't stay long enough to meet the rest of the family, but they were all in Worcester visiting with the O'Tooles that day. I followed him down the path with a sack of early apples.

"For your journey to Boston. Sure I can't wait to see you again! Remember to bring Caitlin after she gets settled."

"I will. She'll be happy to know she has kin in America," he says.

For the first time in years I felt that Ireland and me people were not that far away. I was after hoping I'd be seeing Liam O'Shea again soon. But I haven't seen or heard from him since that day.

Chapter VI.

Paddy Town

The flight of desperate Irish immigrants continued for a few more years, for conditions in Ireland were nearly as harsh from the aftermath as from the Famine itself. But there were many challenges for the Irish in Massachusetts as well. Nana's voice conveyed no small amount of pain as she recalled those years.

Ireland had suffered through a devastating potato famine, but to hear some people talk in Worcester, the city was also suffering from blight: the Famine immigrants. They were crowding into tenements only to find that there was little work to be had on the railroads, so now they were spilling out into the smaller towns to work in the mills.

Cherryfield had four woolen mills that were in need of cheap labor. When we first arrived only Yankees worked in the factories, but now with wages so low the owners were more inclined to hire the Irish. So triple-decker company houses were built near the mills, and they quickly came near to bursting with the large Irish families who called them home.

Your own mother and your Aunt Siobhan went to work in those mills back in '45. Kathleen was only working in them until she found a husband, and didn't she find him right there in the factory? Your father was a weaver in the Joslin Mill. He had eyes for Kathleen Culligan from the very first day she came to work there! That's what he told me, and why shouldn't he fall for her? Sure she was lovely with that chestnut hair. Thanks be to St. Patrick that me daughters didn't take after me for their looks! Both girls were pretty and were always after turning heads.

I remember when we all met your Da. Your Ma'am had only been at Joslin's for a week or two when she showed up one evening with handsome young Frank Haggerty walking alongside her cow-eyed, while your Aunt Siobhan followed them with a mischievous grin! We liked Frank right from the start. He was a real gentleman. He asked Granda straight away if he could walk out with Kathleen. Of course Granda gave his consent. Your mother, being shy, blushed red as wine when Pat and Mike teased her about her "beau." She and Frank were married but six months after they met.

My parents' first child, my brother Sean, was born the next year, in 1848. They would have seven sons. I was their only daughter and their last child, born October 31, 1857. Nana insisted that I was always Granda's favorite, "if the truth be told."

Of course your Aunt Siobhan wasn't the least bit shy. She didn't plan to stay long in the mills. She wanted to attend the high school there in Oxford. Every time she mentioned her scheme your Granda would say to her, "An' where did you get the idea that you could leave a good job just to go stickin' your nose in a lot of books?

But Siobhan was ready to fight about it! "Why shouldn't I go? I don't want to be ignorant all of my life like these *spalpeens* coming over."

She did go off to the high school for a while, but by then she was 20 - a few years older than her classmates. I think she felt out of place, though she'd never admit it. She told us that she missed earning wages and so she left school to go back to the factory. As it turned out, Siobhan was much happier working in the woolen mills and stirring up the workers than reading schoolbooks. Always a firebrand she was, and still is!

But what she said about the new Irish being ignorant wasn't far from the truth, 'though 'twas hardly their fault, seeing as how they were treated by the English. They were not as poor here as they were in Ireland, but they still struggled. Two families would live in a space barely fit for two people. Their children were bullied by their classmates but would get in trouble with the teacher if they fought back. Irish boys were expelled from school and arrested a lot more frequently, it seemed, than the Yankee lads, and Irish fathers and mothers were used to enduring the sneers, cold stares and shut doors of their American neighbors. The poorest of them lived in shacks by the railroad, in what the locals called "Paddy Town."

The Yankees complained about the "rowdy Irish," but we never thought of ourselves that way. Couldn't our neighbors understand that like themselves we were decent people who were only trying to make life better for our children? We worked hard, and at long last had something to show for it.

Barney Culligan had the soul of a farmer and the strength for the work. He was always after ploughing more land and planting more crops so we could sell some of them, and at last we began to make a small profit from our corn as well as our apples. He planned to use the money buy another cow - only that was the summer that our luck started to turn on us.

First, 'twas the hens. I was after finding less and less eggs in the nests. One of the hens disappeared so, and a few others did, too, over the course of three weeks. Granda feared that a fox was after killing our chickens, and he and Pat built a strong fence around the coop.

The morning after the fence was built I went out with Anna to look for eggs.

"What is that, Mama?" She was pointing at the fence.

'Twas a message: "Papists Go Home!" That's what someone had written in charcoal. I had Mike scrub it off afore his father could find it.

Things quieted down for a month or so, but then one day I couldn't find the pig. I searched all over for it, and sent Pat and Mike 'round to ask the neighbors if they'd seen it, but the boys had no luck.

I learned what happened to the poor creature a few days later when I found the pig's head on the doorstep. This time I decided to go to the police.

At the station, the police sergeant was taking a nap and didn't even look up at me when I came into the room.

"Excuse me, sir," I says to him. "I'd like to report a crime."

He opened his eyes and sneered at me, he did. "What is the matter? Is your husband missing? Maybe he's just too drunk to know the way home, Bridget." After all these years me blood still boils when I think of that cop!

"Me husband's fine," I says. "But someone stole our pig and killed it."

He lit up a seegar and smoked it for what must have been a good minute before he answered me.

"How do you know it was killed? Could be that it just wandered off looking for better slop than potatoes."

I wasn't after letting him dismiss me so easily. 'Twas justice I wanted!

"I found its head on my doorstep this mornin', Sergeant," I tells him. "I could bring it in as proof if you'd like!"

He said nothing for a minute, and then he frowned and waved his hand to shoo me away as he might do to a fly.

"Ha! It is probably the work of some of the local toughs. Some sort of prank. You know how it is, Bridget - boys will be boys!"

I could taste the bitter bile in me throat as I answered him.

"Pranks! What kind of a joke is it to destroy a family's winter food? I'd like the names of these 'local toughs'!"

"I have no authority to release any names -" he starts to tell me. Well I wasn't taking any excuses from him!

"An' why not? You have suspects, don't you?"

But the sergeant just shrugged his shoulders.

"Of course not. It could be someone from out of town for all I know. There is enough going on around here with you Irishers drinking and fighting to keep me busy. I know nothing of what goes on with a few young rascals."

'Twas when he said that I realized that there'd be no investigation. "I see now. You know nothing," I says, and I left the police station. I understood him all too well: "Know Nothing." Sure, that's what he was; a member of the hateful Know Nothing Party. Didn't I see the lot of them marching around town in the Fourth of July parade? They were prouder than peacocks as they waved red, white, and blue banners that proclaimed, "America is for Americans."

Many folks have forgotten about them since the War, but years ago the Know Nothing Party was formed to keep immigrants (especially Irish Catholic immigrants) out of America - or at the least, to make it hard for them to stay. The party grew stronger every year since it had begun in the '40s. By the '50s they were running their own candidate for governor of Massachusetts. 'Twas also a fact that in Washington many congressmen were sympathetic to the Know Nothing cause.

The Cherryfield Know Nothings were small in number but strong in their influence over the locals. I heard from some of the newcomers that they often found tenement windows broken and manure flung onto their laundry when it was hanging on the line. Nativist men threatened to have the Irish sent out of town on a rail. They picked fights with our men so that the police would come 'round and put the "Paddies" in jail for disturbing the peace.

Our own peace was nearly disturbed forever that summer.

'Twas the fifth of July. Sure the night was as hot as the day had been. The sheets on the bed were moist and sticky like unbaked bread, and the braid in me hair was soaked with stale sweat. The clock struck ten, eleven, and half-twelve but still I was wide awake, feeling too languid to either toss or turn. 'Twasn't 'til the wee hours that I finally fell asleep, but not for long. I was awakened so about an hour later by a bright light.

I glanced towards the window and saw some sort of illumination. The color put me in mind of a jack o' lantern. Firecrackers, I figured. Some of the neighbor boys probably found a few left over from the Fourth and decided to cause a bit of mischief. Queer, though, that I heard no explosion. Not even a splutter. Something was very odd, indeed. So I got up out of the bed, me heart pounding and me mouth feeling dry as dust. Sure enough, those were no childish rockets out there in the sky.

I could barely speak for the fear of it all. "Barnard! Get up! The barn's afire," I shout.

He awoke at once and called out to Pat and Mike. They stumbled into the room half asleep. The sight from the window woke them up fast, though.

"Our barn's afire, boys. Go fetch some buckets an' go to the river for water, Michael," Granda says. "An' Pat, see if you can fetch some of the neighbors to help."

I ran outside with Anna following sleepily behind me. Mike was already passing a full bucket to his father, and we worked as quickly as we could to put out the flames, but 'twas hopeless. We were lucky (if there was any luck to be had in the situation) that the cows were out to pasture, for the barn was burned to the ground and they would have burned with it. There was naught to do but gather pails of water and pour it on the dry grass to prevent the flames from spreading to the house.

Pat returned after a while with some neighbors who lived near the railroad in Paddy Town. They quickly formed a bucket brigade and spread the water 'round the narrow strip of dry grass that separated the house from the barn. The burning embers of the barn boards were our only light.

The night's stillness had given way to a light summer breeze. At any other time, 'twould be a welcome relief from the stifling heat, but now it became our worst enemy. 'Twas just enough of a wind to carry the flames across the yard and spew smoke into our eyes and noses and mouths. I couldn't see for the darkness, and words were caught in me ash-choked throat. But what could I say when faced with total loss? Anna was sobbing to the point of keening but I could give her no words of comfort. All me effort was turned on saving whatever we could. But there were too many flames and not enough of us to put them out. The fire teased the kitchen lean-to, warning us that we'd best be after leaving before 'twas too late.

Another one of our neighbors, Mr. Thadeus Hill, came to help and worked alongside us until we knew that the battle was lost. "I am so sorry," he says, and I knew he was being sincere. Sure there are some good people in this world. Even amongst the Yankees.

'Twould be later that Pat would tell me other neighbors refused to come. One of them even muttered, "Serves them right. They put on too many airs for Paddies." But I prefer to think about the people who did right by us on that hellish night. It helps to ease the sickening feeling that there are other people out there who want to harm us, just because of where we were born and what we believe.

We knew only too well that if the fire was set, then the devils could very well be still in the neighborhood; so to stay with any of our neighbors would put them at risk of fire as well. Not that there were any offers of shelter. But your Mam and Da took us in for the night.

And didn't we all fell fast asleep, despite the fact that we were lying on a hard floor and we'd just lost our home. Truth be told, I didn't much care to wake up the next morning - or ever. The misery of the night's events haunted me. Granda sat at your Mam's kitchen window, staring out of it as if he could somehow find meaning in such a senseless act if he looked for it long enough in the sooty sky.

As always, Mr. O'Toole was ready to help us. It was half seven the next morning when he knocked on your Mam's door. How the news of the fire traveled to Worcester so fast was a mystery, though Quentin O'Toole could sniff out trouble like a bloodhound.

"I have some rooms you can stay in until the house is repaired," he tells Granda. "Don't worry about the rent; it's my contribution, you might say."

He took us to Worcester in his handsome new carriage - what a grand way to travel! When we arrived at their home, Mrs. O'Toole came down the stairs in her wrapper, yawning. Her long grey hair was usually tucked up neatly under her cap, but on that morning 'twas tied up in a braid that was disheveled from sleep. The good woman raked out the ashes in the stove and made us some tea. We sat down at her kitchen table whilst she bustled about fixing something to eat. She wouldn't hear of any thanks and she wouldn't sit down until we were all stuffed with potatoes and fish cakes, good woman that she was.

"Sure we have to help our own kind. Don't worry. Moira. Mr. O'Toole and the boys will have your house in order in no time," she tells us. She had a comforting way about her, for all of her holiness and domestic perfection.

The next day, Quentin O'Toole took us down to the house so we could survey the damage. Not only the barn but the porch and most of the kitchen were gone. We were after looking for things to salvage, but 'twasn't much to be had. Still, I sifted through the smoke-streaked rubbish in search of treasure. I found a pair of shoes, some sewing scissors, an old medicine bottle, and the creel basket that I'd carried with me from Galway to New York, o'er 25 years before. Inside of it still was the turf I'd taken from our tumbled hearth.

I was after walking out of the house when I saw hanging above the charred kitchen doorway the St. Bridgid's cross.

"Look, Barney! She's still lookin' out for us!"

I tapped Granda's shoulder to show him the cross but he was too dispirited to care.

"Some protection that's given us!" He reached up to grab it, but I stayed his hand, so.

"Please don't tempt our luck," I says. "Let me keep it safe until we return."

"Suit yourself, Woman," he grumbles.

As I took down the cross, Mike and Pat shouted over to us from the remains of the barn.

"All of the animals are accounted for, even the cat and her kittens!" says Mike. He loved all cats, but especially our Pooka, who'd just littered in the last fortnight.

Granda wasn't paying attention to the cats. He had bigger things on his mind. "We'll have to find buyers for the livestock," he says.

Well now, Quentin O'Toole wouldn't hear of that.

"And what will you be doing on the farm all day with no animals to keep?"

Then Granda laughed. There was dark bitterness in it. "I don't think we're allowed to bring our livestock to the poor farm," he says.

Now 'twas Quentin O'Toole's turn to laugh. "Poor farm! Is that where you think you're going? What is the matter with you, Culligan? Sure we'll have this place rebuilt in no time. I was talking to the pastor after early Mass this morning, and didn't I get that old Brit Fr. Gibson to promise me he'll have a work crew from the parish down here by tomorrow! We're all hoping to have you back in here before the snow flies."

Chapter VII.

Home

The family stayed in an apartment owned by Mr. O'Toole while the workers from the church rebuilt the house. "They worked from sun up 'till sun down" Nana recalled. "Mr. and Mrs. O'Toole gave us furniture and the ladies of the church donated clothes and dishes and cooking pots. I felt like a young bride!"

One day during all the rebuilding Siobhan came over to see us. She was still working in the mill at the time. "Mam!" she shouts. "They took up a collection at work today. Look - almost ten dollars!"

Now didn't the tears came to me eyes? "Bless them! An' most of them havin' hardly a penny for their own bread." I was so touched by their kindness.

"Isn't it always the way that those who have the least give the most?" says Siobhan. "I suppose they suffered such great losses themselves during the hunger that it's softened their hearts towards others who suffer."

True indeed, although in Worcester the newer Irish resented those who came before the Hunger for acting too "grand." A gang of them even broke the lace-curtained windows at Toby Boland's house. Quentin O'Toole escaped their wrath since he was after taking them in and finding them jobs, just as he'd done for us so many years afore.

The men from our parish - old Irish and newcomers alike - helped Granda and your uncles work on the house all that summer and into September. Each night Granda would come home from the house-building pleased with the day's progress.

And so one night he came home and told us that we could move back to our farm the next week.

No one worked on the Sunday, of course, and that made Granda all the more eager to get to the house site early Monday morning. I'd barely had time to finish the washing up after breakfast when he returned to Worcester, looking as if all the sorrows of the world were on his heart.

"What' s wrong, machree? Are you sick?" I asks. I'd heard that summer sickness was going around. Granda always hated to be sick, especially since on the farm you still have to take care of things, sick or not.

He sat down at our new kitchen table (given to us by the O'Tooles) and put his head in his hands.

"Tisn't me, 'tis them."

"Who? Mike? Pat? Where are they? Are they all right?" A thousand terrible thoughts swarmed through me head at the very thought of our sons coming down with a sickness or getting hurt on the job.

I could barely believe what Granda told me next.

"No, THEM. The Know-Nothin' Yankees. They - they burned the house again."

"Sure you can't mean it!" But I knew from his face he was speaking the truth. 'Twas just too hard to bear.

"An' would I lie about such a thing, Woman?"

I slipped me arms around him and we held each other for a long time. I didn't cry then. 'Twas still too hard to understand. Why would anyone want to do such a hateful thing? What had we ever done to anyone?

'Twas when I went to the site with the priest that I sobbed. The front room was burned down, although the rest of the house didn't suffer much in the way of damage. Across the charred remains of the porch someone had hung up a banner:

"Go Home! America is for Americans!"

"Why?" I asks Fr. Gibson. Sure he was an immigrant himself, from England.

"I do not know, Mrs. Culligan," he tells me. "Some people just hate us for our faith, or because we are not native born. They fear us because they cannot understand our ways. We must ask God to forgive them and we must forgive them, too."

But 'twould be a long time before I could forgive them, not so much for what they did to the house as for what they did to Granda. He refused to go back, even though Quentin O'Toole promised that 'twas a minor setback and they'd have the house finished in a few weeks' time. "Did ye hear that, Barnard? The men will have this all set to rights an' we'll be going back home soon!"

But he stared at me with the same emptiness in his eyes that I saw in those of the Famine immigrants. I could smell the sickly sweet scent of rum on his breath.

"Home?" he says. "What home? Sure they'll either burn it down again or else make life so miserable for us we'll be after leavin', anyway. We can't beat them, Moira. They'll always win an' we'll always be wanderin' the earth like tinkers."

After that day he spent most of his time in bed, caring for nothing but the next pint of rum. The boys reported on the progress of the house every day. "We'll be in there before the beginning of October, Da," Mike would tell him.

Then one day Pat came back from Cherryfield with some news. "We don't have to worry about anyone burnin' down our barn anymore," he tells us. "The police are searching for the ones who burnt it. Seems the 'pranks' have gone too far this time. The newspapers in Boston have reported on what they did to our house so now it's an embarrassment for the town." 'Twas good that the police finally felt shame.

But I had other concerns - me biggest being Granda. He drank himself sick every night. I asked Dr. Brigham to come in to see him. The doctor closed the door to the room where Granda was sleeping. He spoke in a very low voice, but still I understood what he was telling me - all too well.

"He's suffering from melancholy," the doctor says. "He must get up out of bed, get back to work, and abstain from ardent spirits or his heart could be damaged irrevocably."

That night, I tried to cheer up Granda.

"Quentin O'Toole says he'll give us a ride in his carriage tonight to catch a breeze. 'Tis so hot in here! 'Twouldn't it be grand to get away from the city for a bit? We can go out to Cherryfield an' see the house. Mr. O'Toole says that if you see it, you'll feel so much better about things. 'Tis gettin' done, machree. Have faith," I tell him.

But he was deaf to me words. "Faith! An' what exactly do you mean by that? All these years I had faith that we could get ahead; that as long as we worked hard an' minded our business the Yankees would leave us alone. An' so what happened? Thrown out again, just as we were in Ireland. Don't be talkin' to me about faith, Woman."

I didn't know if anything I'd say to him could get him out of his darkness. Still, I had to try.

"But don't you see, Barnard? If we give up now, they've won. You were the one who kept me goin' when we were evicted from the land all those years ago. Remember? You said, "We'll walk." An' walk we did, an' you got hired for the canal work. An' after all the canal work was done, you kept on lookin' for jobs every day until we got the work with the Brewsters. Sure you never gave up, no matter how many doors were shut in your face. Please don't give up now, machree. I'll not see you killin' yourself for the likes of them that tried to scare us off. We have to be strong like we were years ago, when we left Ireland."

But he just turned his head to the wall. "America is for Americans." He was after muttering that phrase over and over again all day long, as if 'twas part of the Catechism.

For over twenty-five years, I tell you; I'd carried the burden of the work on me back, just like me Mam. But unlike her, for one quarter of a century I'd carried it across an ocean; to paddy camps and tenements and to a small farm that was burned to cinders. I wasn't about to let all those years of toil and dreams be consigned to an ash heap.

"I won't have this!" I says to Granda. "I refuse to give in to them, an' if that's what you're after doin', then yer shamin' us all with your cowardice. 'America for Americans' is it? Well, as they say here, "'I don't buy it!' We're the ones who built their roads an' railways an' canals an' factories, so that they could become rich men in a rich country. We sweep their streets, wash their clothes, dig their ditches, empty their privies, clean their homes, mind their children - an' yet they tell us 'America is for Americans'? An' you're willin' to fall for that lie! Well, do what you like, but I'm goin' back to that house an' that farm an' I'll work the land with or without ye! We'll see who America is for. We've as much a right to that land as anyone else, an' I'll not be hearin' otherwise from anyone - not even yourself, Barnard Culligan!"

His only answer was to pull the blanket over his head.

I was so mad at your Granda, I wouldn't eat or sleep in the same room with him that night or the next!

'Twas the end of that same week when Quentin O'Toole helped us pack up our goods into his cart to take us back to our home. When we got inside the door, the farmhouse was all freshly painted and papered and had the smell of a new house. And there was something else that was new: In the parlor sat a pianoforte!

Now didn't Quentin O'Toole beam with pride when Anna ran her delighted fingers over the keyboard!

"'Twas in a property I purchased in Charlton. 'Tis old but I had it tuned and it plays as well any you'd find in a Boston mansion. I thought you might get some enjoyment from it. My daughter Nora can teach you to play," he says.

Well now, wasn't that a dream come true for our Anna! Quentin O'Toole would be her idol from that day onward.

What a great feeling 'twas so, to be back in me own home - made anew by the work of so many kind hands. I vowed I would never leave that place again until I came out in me coffin!

Sure, 'twas hard for a few years there. Granda kept up the drinking and he showed no inclination to stop. Mike and Pat were now young men and able to do the hardest of chores, but no matter how much they worked, 'twas never good enough for their Da. Of course he himself was often too sick of a morning to do a good day's work, and the guilt was on him for that.

Now Mike himself was strong enough to do the work of two men with nary a complaint. Easygoing he was, but he had the shyness from his mother, truth be told. Oh, how he avoided the women - except for one! Siobhan had a friend, Peg, who worked with her at the mill. Whenever she brought Peg home Mike would stare at her in awe, as if she was the goddess Brigid. But whenever the girl tried to get a word out of him, the poor lad would clam up and excuse himself, muttering that he had chores to do.

So one day Siobhan teased him about his bashfulness after Peg had gone home. "She won't bite, you ninny! Why won't you talk to her?"

Mike said he would try the next time Peg came around. Sure I'd hear him practicing conversations in the barn: "Isn't it a lovely evenin', Peg?" "Would you like a cup of tea, Peg?" "How are your Mam and Da faring, Peg?"

After a month or two, Mike was confident that he could hold his own the next time she came to visit. But wasn't he just beside himself when Siobhan announced that Peg was coming to visit Sunday! Our Mike scrubbed his face and hands 'til they were near to bleeding. He kept his church clothes on after getting home from Mass and wouldn't eat a bite of dinner for fear he'd stain his new shirt. I was thinking he must have combed his hair five or six times while he waited in the parlor, tapping his feet for the nervousness he was after feeling.

Then there came the knock on the door. Mike rose to greet his goddess as Siobhan led her into the room. But the poor lad's smile was short-lived. Peg had come round to show off her new fiancé! After that day, Mike sought no more attention from the ladies.

Just as Kate and Siobhan were opposites, so 'twas with Mike and his brother. Pat was auburn-haired and handsome like his Da, and he had that easy charm with all the lasses. But our Pat didn't play favorites! He was after looking past the pretty faces of the local girls. His heart lay beyond them; beyond the farm and beyond Cherryfield. Sure I'd see him setting down by the river on many an evening, lost in thought. Or else he was after watching the trains leaving the railroad depot, lost in the future. Our world was too small for Pat

Culligan. I could see that, and I knew that some day he would find that out for himself. I only wished that the day wouldn't come too soon. I needed his help on the farm, but I also needed my family to be near - especially since Granda wasn't always so easy to live with in those days. But sure I knew that Pat wouldn't be happy if he stayed at home. 'Tis heartbreaking at times, watching your daughters and sons grow up. Especially when their dreams take them so far from you.

Pat wasn't destined to stay, so, but Mike wouldn't be leaving us. His was a different fate altogether.

'Twas one late June day that the sky threatened to rain. Granda had borrowed Mr. Hill's ox team and cart so that he and the boys could finish the haying. They'd done half a cartload when Mike noticed the gathering of thick, dark clouds. "Sure looks like rain's comin' on soon, Da," he says.

Granda feared that the hay would get wet and spoil.

"Faster, lads! We've not much time to get this done!"

They all worked as fast as the devil, gathering the hay from the fields under the blackening sky. Then the raindrops started to fall. Granda was wanting to drive the hay cart into the barn before it got too wet, so he yells to Mike, "Go over and open the barn an' be quick about it!"

Mike ran on ahead to open the barn door whilst Pat jumped up onto the wagon seat and Granda gave the oxen a flick of the switch. The beasts hurried down the path so quick that they nearly turned the cart on its side. Poor Mike didn't make it to the barn in time. Indeed, he was after running so fast he slipped on the wet grass and fell just in time for the oxen to drive over him.

"HELP!!!!!" Mike yelled out with all of his strength. But the damage was done. His left leg was twisted like rope.

Pat shouted in Granda's ear. "Fetch the doctor, Da!" But 'twas Pat who ran off on the errand, while Granda stayed with Mike, giving him sips of rum.

When Dr. Brigham came he and Pat lifted Mike onto the wet hay cart and brought him back to the house. It took a

very large bottle of rum to ease the pain as the doctor set the broken bones. Mike was given laudanum that night and he slept peacefully, but 'twould be many weeks before he could walk again, and then only with a cane. Sure he's been lame from that time to this.

Granda felt terrible about the accident. At first, he tried to forget about it in his usual manner - by drinking. He left Pat and meself to do most of the work, and one day I was so tired from helping with the ploughing that I collapsed right in the middle of the field and couldn't get up for the exhaustion I was after feeling.

That did it for Pat. He carried me into the house and called to Granda, "Come and see what you've done to Mam! It's a wonder she isn't dead."

Granda shuffled into the parlor, where I lay on the sofa. I recall that I was after feeling too weak to even raise me head to look at him.

Pat says to him, "If you'd spend more time on the job and less time with the drink, she wouldn't be so worn out, doing your work as well as her own!"

Well, I hate to recollect it even to this day, but your Granda struck Pat so hard across the mouth that lad spat out more than one tooth. But Pat had a temper to match his Da's, and he hit Granda back, right in the gob.

"Is this how ye treat yer own father?" Granda asks him.

But Pat was still angry.

"And is this how you treat your own wife - working her to the bone? It's an early grave you're sending her to. Just look at her, open your bloodshot eyes and take a good look at Mam!"

This time Granda didn't lash out at his son. Instead, he walked over to me and really studied me face, as if he hadn't ever seen me before. He reached out to touch me, but instead - perhaps because I was after lookin' like Death Himself, he knelt at me side and held me hand.

"I'm sorry, mavourneen," he says. A tear was sliding down his cheek.

I didn't answer. 'Twasn't out of bitterness, but because I felt too tired to open me mouth and say anything. That tired feeling wasn't just the result of the day's work but of all the years I labored to keep our farm and our family together. I just kept me hand in Granda's as I fell asleep.

The very next day, Granda stopped drinking for good. He worked hard on the farm after that and he treated me like royalty. I never had to lift anything heavier than a kitten. He'd carry the laundry baskets as well as the milk pails. Life on the farm was good again.

But as I mentioned afore, your Uncle Pat had set his sights on things far beyond Cherryfield, Massachusetts. 'Twas the day after his 25th birthday that he says to us, "I've been thinking there might be more opportunity for me in the West. They need strong men out there and I don't think they'd be against hiring Irish, so I'm heading out to Nebraska. That's where the real America is: in the West. A man can get land and start a new life for himself in Nebraska, and that's what I intend to do."

Granda wasn't happy to hear all that. He thought Uncle Pat was being selfish. "An' so you're after leavin' us here, with your brother an' me havin' to do your share of the work as well as our own? Is that any way to show your gratitude to your own Mam an' Da?"

I wasn't after letting guilt keep Pat from following his dreams, so I says to Granda, "An' why shouldn't he go? Mike can get around all right; sure he can take over Pat's chores, an' Frank will help us if we need it. The lad's right, I'm thinkin'. Maybe in the West they won't care if he's Catholic. He can make a decent livin'."

Granda knew I was right, so he says to Pat, "Go on, so, with our blessin' son."

I felt as if the heart was being ripped out of me chest on that day we saw Pat off at the railway station. I held onto him as long as I could. How the years fly! One minute a babe, the next, a young man whose eyes revealed the excitement he was after feeling for his new adventure. And so I had to let him go. He might as well have gone to the moon, for I've never seen him again in the flesh. I only have photographs to bring him back to me for a minute or two.

Now the photograph of your Uncle Pat that you see there on top of the piano is the one of him in his soldier's uniform, taken during the war. The day we got the letter from him telling us that he enlisted was the beginning of the end for your Granda.

"Sure he'll never return." He'd say that every night after we finished with the Rosary. His favorite cousin had to fight with the English army during the wars with Napoleon, and his death was one of Granda's worst childhood memories.

"We can only pray to the Blessed Mother for his safety," I'd tell him, and indeed, our prayers were answered. Not only did Pat escape harm, but he met a young widow lady along the way and they were married before the war was over.

Your own Da couldn't join up because of his hearing being damaged from working in the mill, and Mike had to stay out of it, being that he was lame. But we'd be making our own sacrifice for the Union. Siobhan's husband, Tom, enlisted. He was a strong healthy man. Fit for the soldiering life Tom was. Siobhan and he had met when she was on strike at Joslin's mill. The mill owners were goading the strikers to get back inside, and a few of them did, but not your aunt! She refused to move off the steps of the factory. "Not until we get decent wages," she says to a foreman. The foreman was a handsome Kerryman named Thomas Doyle. Siobhan took one hard look at Mr. Doyle, and she knew the course of her future - and his.

'Twas the foreman's duty to take Siobhan by the arm and either lead her back inside or else show her the gate. But Mr. Doyle was just as thunderstruck. He took her by the arm and took her out past the gate and down the road.

"Where do you think you're takin' me?" Siobhan asks him.

So Tom Doyle says, "I'm takin' you home." But he didn't take her home to the farm. Tom brought her to his own home where his mam served up a mutton dinner. Both mother and son were taken with Siobhan, despite her sharp tongue. And so the following November Siobhan and Tom were wed. A queer couple they were, for he was always after fretting about abiding by the law, and she was after breaking the rules - any rules. She went on strike at every mill she worked at until she was blackballed from them all.

Now would me feisty daughter decide to stay home and keep the house for her man? Indeed not! She didn't have children to care for so she had plenty of time for mischief, and she joined one of those women's rights groups, the kind that hold demonstrations. Her own husband was forever bailing her out of jail!

"Siobhan, darlin'," Tom would say to her. "How do you think this looks, yourself stirrin' things up an' gettin' arrested? Sure it's all the lads talk about down at the mill."

But she would dismiss Tom's pleadings every time. "Who cares what it looks like? I'll do what I think is right!" And the poor man couldn't do a thing about it!

Siobhan was all for her man going into the war. "I'd be going there, too, if a woman could take up arms," she'd tell him. "We have to put those rebs in their place!"

Tom was reluctant to go, at first. For didn't he just get a healthy rise in wages as a foreman at the new carpet mill? Besides, he was 37 at the time. "Let the younger men go," he'd say. But Siobhan's appeals to his patriotism eventually convinced him to enlist. Oh, how she kissed and embraced him when the day came for his leaving! I thought she'd smother the poor man! And then didn't she cry buckets when the train disappeared down the tracks.

There was naught to do but to throw herself into helping the soldiers in any way she could. Siobhan made bandages and sent food and clothes not just to her own husband but to any man from Cherryfield who was in the army. She even organized socials with the Yankee ladies who were raising funds for the war effort. There was no woman in Cherryfield - or maybe even in all of Massachusetts - who was more proud of her husband than Siobhan Doyle.

Then the black day came when the telegram arrived, telling us that Corporal Doyle had been killed at Vicksburg. That proud young woman who refused to cry whenever she got the switch as a child was now nearly breathless from keening. That night I held her in me lap and rocked her to sleep, just as I'd done when she was a baby.

So Siobhan came to live with us again. A blessing she was, because I was too busy caring for Granda to tend to the housework. Ever since the war broke out, he found it difficult to sleep for worry over Pat and Tom. He was bone-weary, too, from all of the hard work he'd done over the years. Even back in his drinking days - excepting for the time in the Lunatic Asylum - he always stayed on the job. Now he could barely pick up a shovel without gasping for breath. When old Dr. Brigham came to visit he was shocked by Granda's appearance. Me poor man had lost a lot of weight and was no longer brawny. Even his stature seemed crimped.

After the doctor examined Granda, he told me the bad news: "Dropsy of the heart, Mrs. Culligan. I fear that he might not be here by harvest season." All we could do was make him comfortable as possible and see to it that he had peace and quiet.

Not that it was ever quiet in our house! About a month after Siobhan came home to live, a carriage pulled up in front of the gate, and out of it stepped a fair-haired young man in a soldier's uniform. And didn't me heart nearly jumped to me mouth, for fear that the soldier had bad news to impart about Pat!

Thanks be to God! 'Twasn't about Pat. In fact, 'twas a pleasant surprise when the young man introduced himself as Otto Mueller from Lockport, New York.

"Mr. Culligan worked together with my grandfather on the Erie Canal," he says to me.

"Indeed he did! Well come right in, so. We'll be wantin' to hear about your Grandmam an' Granda," I tells him.

So Otto followed me inside and didn't Granda's face light up when young Mr. Mueller told him how his grandparents would often talk about their Irish friends, the Culligans!

"They passed away five years ago, but I never forgot their stories," he tells us. "So when my unit came here to Massachusetts, I decided to look for you. I called upon the priest in Worcester and he directed me here."

Mr. Mueller was a well-spoken young man. He was a devout Catholic, too, and he attended Mass with us the next Sunday before going back to Boston to rejoin his unit. Every day of his short leave he'd had dinner with us, and in the evenings he would play the piano whilst Anna joined him in the latest ballads. 'Twas a pleasant time for us all.

When it was time for his departure we thought that would be the last we'd be seeing of Otto Mueller, but weren't we wrong! He and Anna commenced to writing to each other, with the envelopes getting thicker by the week, and 'twasn't long until Anna would run out first every day to fetch the mail. On some days she'd be after blushing when she came back, holding another precious letter to her bosom.

The following winter, a letter arrived addressed not to Anna but to Granda. He asked me to read it to him, but we both knew what it was about before we even looked at the contents: Otto Mueller declared his love for our girl, and he was after asking for Granda's permission to marry Anna. Of course, he'd secretly asked Anna to wed him many months before that, permission or not!

'Twas in March of 1864 that Mr. Mueller came back to Cherryfield with two day's leave, and he and Anna were married in St. John's. Sure, I'd always thought Anna would marry one of our own, an Irishman, but Otto's been a good husband and a good provider for her. 'Tis lovely having them and their children living on a farm so close to our own.

After the wedding, Quentin O'Toole drove us back to our house and we had quite a hooley! You could barely move between the kitchen and the parlor, 'twas that crowded. Besides our family, there were a few soldier friends of Otto's and at least a dozen O'Tooles. Quentin's daughter Nora played waltzes and polkas on the piano and had many a guest tapping a foot. Anna even managed to coax Granda into a lively gallop! He moaned and groaned whilst she led him around the parlor but he was smiling, he was. Still, it took him two weeks of bed rest to recover from the all the excitement!

Granda didn't go out much from December 'til the end of February. All winter long he was after talking to Mike and your Da about the crops he planned to grow. 'Twas a long winter; that last one of the war, and it seemed forever until spring came and so 'twas planting time again.

Early spring was always Granda's favorite time on the farm. He loved to plough, 'though the rocks in the soil would threaten his blade. Every day, rain or shine, he'd be after walking through our fields, coaxing the plants to grow - his "babies" he called them.

But that spring he was too weak to work the land. Mike and your Da did the planting, and on warm days in early April we'd bring out a chair for Granda so he could supervise the work. As in years past, he had plenty of orders to give out.

"Mike, now, be sure to add a lot of manure this time around."

"Frank, I think the row is too close."

"Mind the rocks, lads!"

On some evenings if he felt well enough I would walk him out to the orchard so that he could smell the new green grass and admire the budding apple blossoms. One evening, a pink and lavender sunset put me in mind of a of a Galway spring.

That night before we went to bed I asks him, "Do you ever miss home, machree?"

He squeezed me hand whilst grinning like an imp. "What are ye talkin' about, mavourneen? Don't ye remember what I said to ye when we landed in New York all those years ago? 'From now on this is our home,' I says. An' if it wasn't for all of your dreamin' and schemin' to get us this house, well, we wouldn't have a place to call our own now, would we? You're the one to thank for this, Moira Culligan. An' where would I be without ye, Woman!"

And where would I have been without him, I wondered? For all of his stubbornness and struggles against the drink and the Yankees, he had given me a new life in a new land, and I loved him all the more for that.

In April, the terrible war finally came to a close. My Aunt Anna received a telegram that very day from Uncle Otto, telling her that he would be home soon. I remember how she danced with me around the kitchen until Nana hushed us because Granda was trying to rest. I was only a little girl but I recall the excitement of that day. The mills closed early so that everyone could watch the parade that the Mexican War veterans had organized, and that night there were parties and fireworks all over town. But Nana's recollections of the war's end differed greatly from those of a child's.

The day that the war ended there was a grand celebration in Cherryfield. Rockets and Roman candles showered the April skies that night. You'd never know 'twas Holy Week for all the giddiness. We all sat out on the porch to watch the fireworks, despite the chilly spring air. Well, almost all of us. Mike had joined Quentin O'Toole and your Da in a boat ride along the river. Your Mam was after saying, "Frank will catch his death of cold, the great fool!"

"Oh, stop being such a ninny, Kate!" Siobhan says to her. "This is a night to celebrate! We can get back to fightin' for other important things now that the war is over - like getting women the right to vote."

Granda grumbled a little but he knew better from times past than to argue with Siobhan about women's rights!

Anna was after weeping for joy. "I'm just so happy that Otto will be coming home alive -" She would have said a lot more, but she noticed the tears in Siobhan's eyes and apologized to her for being inconsiderate.

But Siobhan, that big-hearted girl, gave Anna a kiss on the forehead. "I'm glad he'll be coming home, too, little sister," she says. "You caught yourself a good one - even if he isn't Irish!" 'Twasn't it just like Siobhan to tease her sister despite her own sorrow.

I was after listening to the peepers singing by the pond. 'Twas as if as if they, too, were happy that the war was over.

"Peace at last," I says to your Granda.

I had wrapped him up in two blankets and a quilt. He was enjoying the evening, but as soon as the last rocket was fired he says, "I'm after goin' to bed now. I'm in sore need of a rest." Your mam helped him into his bed. She said he fell asleep as soon as his head met the pillow.

When I came into the bed a while later, I saw that he was sleeping like a baby. I tried to get under the covers quietly, so as not to wake him, but he opened his eyes and grasped for me hand.

"Is that you, Moira?"

"*Sea*, machree. Can I get you anythin'?"

"No, mavourneen, just - just stay close."

We held hands while the fear took ahold of me so. His hand felt clammy, and his breathing was shallow.

"Put your head on me shoulder, Moira, like you used to do when we were young," he tells me.

I leaned down onto his shoulder very carefully, because he'd become so thin and looked so brittle.

He was whispering to me, very soft-like. "*Sea*, that's better. That's me girl. You know, mavourneen, as soon as I saw you that day, hidin' behind the bushes, I knew you were the one."

Didn't I blush so, like a maiden! He'd seen me on that Beltane morning long ago, when I'd peeked at him from me hiding place, as I scrambled to put on me clothes!

"I never knew you noticed me that time," I says to him. And didn't I still blush at the memory, after all those years!

He tried to laugh, but coughed from the effort. "Of course I noticed ye! Why do ye think I sought you out? What a pleasin' sight you were indeed - an didn't I know somethin' about lovely lasses!"

"You've always been a bit of a devil, Barney Culligan, but I wouldn't have you any other way." I says, and I leaned over to kiss him, so. He looked at me with such love in those old eyes that still reflected the green hills of Connemara.

"*Moira, ta gra oram roit...* I love you..." His voice faded away, so - and he was gone from me.

Nana lived for 10 years after Granda's passing. Uncle Mike, who never married, has stayed on at the farm with Aunt Siobhan, who never re-married. She remains an ardent advocate for women's suffrage.

Bridget's Home

I visited my grandmother many times after our interviews had ended. We would talk about her flower garden, the latest letter from my Uncle Pat and other cheerful topics, but never again about the past.

Last Easter Nana suffered a stroke. When I came down to see her the following day she had already slipped into a coma. A week later, while briefly regaining consciousness, she whispered, "I'll be goin', so," – and died.

About the Author:

Katie M. Hill has written three plays about 19th century Irish immigration. Bridget's Home is based on the first play of her Immigrant Trilogy, which also includes stories of the Famine and post-Famine Irish. In addition to researching and offering programs about the Irish Diaspora, Ms. Hill frequently portrays Mary Culligan at Old Sturbridge Village.

Made in the USA
Middletown, DE
13 December 2015